愛 在 瘟 疫 時
Love in the
Time of Coronavirus

何福仁詩集
Tran. by Teresa Shen

匯智出版

目錄

愛在瘟疫時

我只能讚美你的眼睛
隔着眼鏡我仍然看到
那雙晶瑩流轉的寶石
我本來也想讚美
你油亮的美髮
你那挺直自信的鼻子
你一定也有張暖紅的嘴唇
整齊潔白的牙齒
但我只能想像
用浮泛的修辭
因為都躲在頭套、口罩裏
我聽不清你的説話
你的眼神，充滿疑惑
又為甚麼這樣憂傷？

Love in the Time of Coronavirus

I cannot help but admire your eyes
Through my glasses I can still make out
twin gems sparkling in their luminosity
I want to admire
the luster in your hair
the poise and sureness of your nose
or the warm rosy lips you must possess

complete with tidy sparkling teeth

But I can only imagine

in rhetoric too shifty and shy

Hidden under headgear and mask

I cannot make out your words

But your eyes, full of misgiving

full of sadness, why?

把你收藏在口罩裏

我把你收藏在口罩裏
安全、溫暖
這是局部封關
進出都要保持距離
距離就是，封是封不了
還有那雙看路的眼睛
一左一右的耳朵
不斷清洗的十隻指頭
只是要你輕緩地呼吸
不再亂説話
不再拌嘴
也不再親嘴
交換唾液
是危險的行為
會把你出賣
會把一個偉大的朝代
坑了

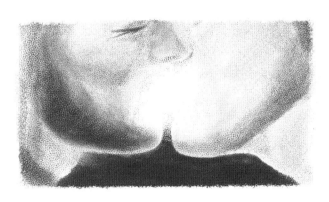

Keeping you in my mask

I keep you inside my mask
snug and warm
This is only partial quarantine
to maintain a safe distance out, a safe distance in
Only partial closure, complete lock-down is out,
for the eyes that watch the road ahead
for the ears on either side of your head
and for the ten fingers constantly being washed
All you need to do is to breathe slowly
Watch what you say
No more contraries
No more kisses
Any exchange of saliva is
a deeply dangerous act
It could betray you
It could push a great dynasty
over the edge

禁忌的名字

它有膚色、性別？
有國籍？
它令大人又害怕又要看
看了又看
不知看出甚麼？
我們呢，要閉嘴
因為不可說
不可說，難道就等於不存在？

老師責備我不肯乖乖坐定
它呢，它不是跑來跑去
跑出課室外
坐郵輪，乘直通車
跑到東，跑到西
還搭飛機
周遊世界去
好像只有它才可以自由地遊戲
跑出說話的禁區

為了它的降臨
城市洗了又洗
噴滿了怪異的香水
因為它會穿牆，會爬水渠
在空氣裏？
它令老人家排隊兩個小時

為了兩個口罩，像中了彩
它令人不敢打麻將，不敢吃火鍋
到超市去搶米，搶潔手液
又不是不用錢，而且
都漲價了
最奇怪的是
爸媽搶那麼多的廁紙，難道
它藏了很大很大的殺傷武器
在廁所裏？
還在拼圖的嫌犯
已先定了罪

那一次
我無意中說出它的名字
被老師記了大過
因為我把所有人都嚇瘋了
再犯，肯定掃出校門

IT, who must not be named

What skin colour is IT? What gender?
What nationality?
To adults, IT's scary, and piques their curiosity
Curiouser and curiouser
Yet, no one can have IT deciphered
For us, we keep our mouth shut
Because we mustn't say

Mustn't say, but it doesn't mean it isn't here to stay

The teacher chastised me for wriggling about
IT, though, has no restraint
IT runs away from the classroom
Goes on liners, on through-trains
From East to West
Taking a flight too
And goes on a world tour
As if IT alone has the liberty to go on a spree
outside the quarantine of languages

To prepare for IT's visit
cities are washed and rinsed
and sprayed with unusual fragrance
Because IT can go through walls and climb up pipes
and in our air IT presides?
IT makes old folks wait in line for 2 hours or more
Jubilant, like winning the lotteries, to get 2 face masks
IT makes people afraid of mahjong games and hotpot get-togethers
Storm supermarkets for more rice and hand sanitizers
as though they are free of charge. Really
the prices have gone up much more
But the weirdest of it all
was Mom and Dad amassing toilet rolls
Perhaps IT has stashed some lethal weapons
at toilets around the city
The criminal whose profile is still being compiled

is already found guilty

One time
I let its name slip out from my lips
and received from the teacher a warning
for terrifying everyone at school
A second offense will have me kicked out for sure

瘟疫心理學

瘟疫是個心理學的問題
一位心理學家説
他是個棄嬰
由某種蝙蝠領養
在孤獨裏長大
長期受壓抑
見不得光
自閉，也不免自戀
這方面他其實近女性
經過科學的驗證，他斷定
所有女作家都有幽懼症
男性呢，會成為昇華
成為藝術家
難怪當他遇到同類
（他以為是同類
由於共同的口味
共同的性取向）
就廝磨好一陣
如此這麼的一種愛
到了盡頭就是恨
心理學家眼泛淚光：
當天亮時
不得不分開
也就一個生離
一個死別

Pandemic psychology

Pandemic is a psychological condition
says a psychologist:
It is an abandoned child
adopted by some kind of bat
Raised in seclusion
in extensive inhibition
No lights at all
Autistic, and unavoidably narcissistic
it is really more feminine in this regard
He concludes, with evidence most scientific
that all female writers are claustrophobic
Male, on the other hand, will become
masters in their field
It is no surprise that when it meets its kind
(or it deems to be its kind
based on similar inclination
or sexual orientation)
they become intimate
But love of this nature
invariably ends in hate
In teary eyes, the psychologist says:
Separate they must
at sunrise
one dies
the other survives

怎麼過得了關？

怎麼過得了關？
申報時訛稱來源
虛報年齡，多少歲月
無數戰火走過
體溫恆常
逃過智能測謊機
行李輕得都放到肚皮裏
擁有環球護照
樣貌，讓人只看到自己

怎麼就過了關
住進我們的社區
馬上建立龐大的網絡？
原來打通了守關的舌尖
最脆弱的防線
嘴巴不愛錢，只嗜野味
喜歡和其他嘴巴飲宴
烤蝙蝠，梨片伴蒸
果子狸

How did it get past?

How did it get past?
Faked its origin at declaration

Lied about its age; for many months and years
and countless battles, it has traversed
in constant body temperature
It evaded the most intelligent lie detector
and carried luggage small enough to hide in the tummy
It owned passports from nations all over
It looked no more or less than the holder

How did it get past?
How into our communities it entered
and built at once an extensive network?
Sadly, the tongue, our guard, was compromised
The weakest link in our defense
The tongue had no taste for money, indulged only in game
Together with fellow tongues it gathered to feast
on roasted bat and stewed pear
with civet cat

在太陽下面它沒有影子

在太陽下面它沒有影子
它說不要有光
就不再有光
它在鏡子裏看到一副猙獰的面目
大驚，從此把自己收藏
並且不時化裝易容
有時成為少女，成為保安
成為乞丐，成為首相
它悄悄地出席宴會，它喜歡
流連地攤、菜市場
看見娃娃魚，它會游泳
看見雀鳥，它會飛翔
它是這樣暗暗地愛上人類
好奇，耽新，不怕冒險的人類
難得不知道自己是這樣被愛着
終有一天，它想，他們是會明白的：
我寬恕他們的無知，欣賞他們的單純
它尤其喜歡成為長者
乘車、坐船都獲得減價
又都得到特別照顧：扶持、讓座
它跑到護老院探訪
又參觀愈來愈多的劏房
太好了，它就怕寂寞
它走過一個又一個城市觀光
發誓要成為永久的人類

説他們地道的語言
吃他們的風味
膜拜他們的神祇
誰知道這就引起騷動
人們紛紛關起了門戶
戴上了面具，互不信任
親朋戚友不相聚
它成為歹毒的轉喻
向它潑酒精、灌肥皂水
還在研製可怕的針藥
它想：我做過甚麼呢
因為深沉的愛？

No shadow under the sun

It has no shadow under the sun
It says: let there be no light
And there is no more light
It once caught its own reflection, a hideous, monstrous face
Shocked, it has been hiding itself ever since
It changes appearance often
Sometimes it is a young girl, or a watchman
Sometimes a beggar, or a prime minister
Quietly it attends dinner parties; It likes
street stores and vegetable markets
watching salamanders swim
watching birds fly by

It has fallen in love, secretly, with mankind
These inquisitive, audacious, adventurous people
Oblivious, for now, to how much they are loved
One day, eventually, they will understand, it muses,
I forgive them for their ignorance, appreciate their innocence
It especially likes being the elderly
with their bus and ferry concessions
and special treatments: extra support and priority seats
It pays visits to elderly homes
and numerous subdivided housing units
So delighted, a lover of companies
sightseeing it goes from one city to the next
It vows to become one of the humans
speak their dialects
eat their favourites
and pray to their deities
But who'd ever expect with such upheaval they react
They shut their doors and windows
Put on masks and turn distrustful
Stop seeing friends and families
Turn it into the symbol of all things harmful
Douse it with alcohol and soapy water
and develop terrible injections to pierce its skin
It puzzles: What have I done to deserve this?
Because I love them dearly?

病毒醫生

有一天，他脫下口罩
發覺原來沒有鼻子
沒有嘴巴

沒有嘴巴
那是因為說了不該說的話
損害了免疫系統

但為甚麼沒有鼻子呢
原來已沒有了呼吸
他也不能免疫

還好他留下了見證
那一雙炯炯有神的眼睛

Dr Pandemic

One day, he took off his face mask
and found no nose
nor mouth

There was no mouth
because he'd said something he shouldn't have
He disturbed the immune system

But why wasn't there a nose?
because he had stopped breathing
He had no immunity

Thank goodness there were his eyes
The clear, steadfast eyes where truth resides

病船

一艘船病了
據說會傳染另一艘船
沒有一個島讓它停泊
島與島都在地圖上
逐一消失
沒有燈塔
它一直漂泊
倦得長出了苔蘚
長出了蹼
因為長期戴上口罩
只能用鰓呼吸
但沒有一尾魚當它是同類
連蝦毛也沒有

可憐啊，一個漁夫在岸上說
可別把海也污染了

Sick Ship

A ship is sick
It may infect other ships, it seems
No island allows it to berth
Island after island disappears
from the map

No lighthouse either

It keeps wandering

drifting, wearily, till kelps grow hither

Webs develop too

Extended use of mask

makes gills the only way to breathe

But no fish consider it their kind

not even the humble plankton

Poor thing, a fisherman observes from the shore

Please, don't pollute the ocean

豈曰無衣

上陣了，怎能説沒有防毒面具
讓我的和你共用
病毒已經瀰漫，戴上
也沒有意思，就打開城門吧
我們反守為攻

修好甲胄與戈矛，進入戰場
怎能説沒有後援
我不是和你一起麼
我們相濡以沫
互相保護

開戰了，怎能説沒有軍裝
把我的和你分享
我們一起取暖
一起對抗，那怕
一起陣亡

How can you say you are unarmed?

On the frontline, how can you say you have no masks
Let us share mine
The virus has spread in the air, putting on masks
is pointless. Let us open the gate

We counter attack

Breastplate and spear at the ready, into the field we go
How can you say you have no backup?
Am I not your Band of Brothers
Let us stay together
and watch each other's back

In battle, how can you say you have no armour
Let us use mine
We stay warm together
We fight hand in hand, or
vanquish together

Translator's note:
豈曰無衣 is an allusion to the poem 無衣 from the Book of Songs (詩經) of 11th BC to 7th BC, Odes of Qin (秦風).

搓手戀

搓子之手，本可以偕老
我原也出身良好
冰清玉潔
九成九免於毒素
無奈殘留瑕隙
受後母利用
把我騙賣到火坑
鴇母以為奇貨可居
轉借奸商圖利
公子啊，既然金盡床頭
還不快快上京
別再流連柳巷
別鎮日買醉
發憤讀書
一朝高中
回來為我贖身
清洗歹毒
更別移情別戀
成為駙馬
像所有的輕薄兒
那麼我化為青煙
也不會把你放過

Ode of a Hand Sanitizer

Rubbing your hands, I could have grown old along with you
From a decent family I was raised
a woman of innocence and virtue I stayed
99% virus-free
Alas, the trace toxin in me
made me fall prey to my step-mother
who vended me to a brothel
Madam the keeper saw in me a rare commodity
And traded me with profiteers for more pennies
Dear sir, if you could spend no more on me
Why don't you head to the capital city
and stay away from places raunchy and filthy?
Why don't you work on your studies
and lay off the drinking parties?
One day you will prosper
You will return to buy my freedom
You will wash away all my venom
But should you be fickle
and marry up for convenience
like all these frivolous fellows
I promise, even if I am no more
I will return to even the score

Translator's note:
搓子之手 is an allusion to the poem 擊鼓 from the Odes of Bei (邶風) collection in the Book of Songs (詩經) of 11th BC to 7th BC.

悠悠我心

親愛的，我的電腦也沾上了病毒
我只能寫信
這方面我笨劣粗疏
不借助機械
卻是人與人最直接最親切的接觸
只是你看信時，別忘了消毒
我當然也可以打電話
只是想到按了七次不同的編號
然後再選擇政治、經濟、宗教、心理……
走出了迷宮，終於
接通愛情部門，竟又要分別
同性戀、異性戀、雙性戀、畸戀、失戀
老天，我儘在做壞事
可沒有一件成功

我還是重新學用文字符號
重新學習溝通
世間有這麼多的區別
即使毫無徵兆
也會把我們隔離十四天
那是二千一百四十分鐘
八萬六千四百秒
愛情，難道像食物
可以冷藏，添加防腐
情人呢，睡進休眠艙？

我是多麼多麼想念你啊
你也想念我麼？
我無法翻牆找你
你為甚麼不能捎我音訊
別信謠言，那許多的駭客
那許多的監控
別聽姨媽姑爹的挑撥
那許多的暴發戶
我們的姻緣前訂
公平，對等
豈同貿易談判
感情不是價格
經得起時空的考驗
至少維持五十年
至少，不由於一場疫症

The holiness of the Heart's affections

My dearest, my computer has also gotten the virus
I can only write you a letter
I am no good with computers
Without technology
a letter is the closest, most direct contact
Just don't forget to sanitize it before you read
I could telephone, I admit
But the thought of pressing codes in sets of 7
to pick under politics, finance, religion, psychological condition…

One maze after another, to get through

at last, to the department of Love, only to find more options:

Homosexual, heterosexual, bi-sexual, illicit-sexual, devoid-of-sexual

Alas, these wicked deeds I had all done

None of them successful

I'd better learn again the symbols of words

and the code of communication

Our world is full of different systems

Even without symptoms

we could be isolated and separated for 14 days

That's 2,140 minutes

86,400 seconds

Can love, like food

be frozen, for preservation?

And lovers sent to Hibernation?

I so very much miss you

Do you miss me?

I cannot reach you climbing the Firewall

Can you not send me Messages?

Don't fall for fake news; there are all these hackers

all these tracking and monitoring

Don't heed insinuations from any Tom, Dick and Harry

and all those nouveau-riche

Our love is our destiny

Compatibility, equality

Love is not a trade talk

Feelings have no price tags

Our love will stand the test of time

for no less than 50 years

Or, last for at least one pandemic

Translator's note:

The title 悠悠我心 is from 子衿, one of the poems in Odes of Zheng (鄭風) in the Book of Songs (詩經) of 11th BC to 7th BC. The English translation alludes to John Keats, Letter to Benjamin Bailey, *"I am certain of nothing but of the holiness of the Heart's affections and the truth of the imagination"*.

瘋劫

真是世風淪喪
老子當年劫銀行，搶金鋪
手抱霰彈槍，大氣磅礡
到時釋放幾隻灰鴿
完美地詮釋暴力美學
策劃了大半年
因為一場疫症並沒有實踐
苦難當前，警匪無分界線
如今呢，三個小子拎了小刀
跑進超市
打劫甚麼呢？
廁紙

數十卷廁紙，市值一千數百元
還需租借迷你倉儲存
同樣一場疫症
卻丟盡了這行當
多年來竊國封侯的美譽
是沒有口罩可搶
退而求其次？抑或
是受僱推銷
假傳廁紙斷缺？
還是都壞了肚子
凌凌淋淋
要不停如廁？

Batty Heist

What has the world come to
Our lot robbed banks, jumped jewelers
Shotguns at the ready, pizzazz no less
We'd let go of a few doves, for effect
Called it Aestheticization of Violence
The heist, planned for almost a year
now called off due to the virus
In hard times, cops are thugs and thugs are cops
But now, three lowlifes with pocket knives
a supermarket they plundered
What for?
Toilet paper

Toilet rolls in the dozens, may be worth a couple of thousands
Not to mention storage requirement
An epidemic is hardly finished
but the hard-earned respect
of our age-old profession, tarnished
Was it because there were no face masks to steal?
Toilet rolls were the second best? Were they
hired to create a run
A toilet paper marketing push? Or
A real case of tummy runs
lickety-split
using up rolls like it will never be done?

忘情

上一次瘟疫才不過十七年
怎麼我竟渾忘了
曾否為口罩
為酒精潔手液頻撲？
我曾否神經質地搶購廁紙？
每天洗手二三十次
不敢和朋友聚會
不再到電影院去？
那時小花還在
牠會像如今的妹妹
奇怪我成為了宅男
獸子那樣，跟牠一起看着窗外？
日出日落，昨天才分手
怎麼我已絕情地記不起來
政府曾否宣稱全球採購口罩
兩個多月過去，仍然在加油？
它曾否在郵輪上肆虐？
在疫城，滯留的人
在苦苦待救？
肯定的是，醫護人員
沒曾投訴裝備不足
七八個殉職
更沒有人侈言
會牢牢記住一本賬簿
這筆賬，何不等到最後審判？

悲哀不是疫症
而是我竟渾忘過去
失憶，難道是家族遺傳
這一場瘟疫沒有受控
我已經憂慮下一場到來

Forgotten

Only 17 years it has been since the last epidemic

How come I have no recollection?

Did I go berserk over face masks

and alcohol sanitizers?

Did I go crazy stockpiling toilet paper

washing hands twenty, thirty times a day

too scared to meet friends

or go to cinemas again?

If my Fa-fa were still around

would she not, like Mui-Mui now, find it odd

that I have turned into an Otaku, a dull home-stayer

watching, with her, the world outside the window?

Day in and day out; only yesterday did we part

How come I become so unfeeling, so forgetful?

Did the government announce global mask procurement

and was still mouthing slogans two months after the announcement?

Did the virus ravage cruise liners?

Were people stranded in fallen cities

waiting to be released?

I am certain though; not one medical worker ever
complained about the lack of equipment
Half a dozen dead on the job
Yet no one proclaimed
that one day these debts would be claimed
These accounts; why not settle on Judgment Day?
I grieve not for the pandemic
I grieve because I forget
Could amnesia be hereditary?
This pandemic is still ravaging
and I worry about the next

加拿大來郵

弟弟，不用再寄口罩
我戴了口罩到公園散步
其他人，都對我投以奇異的眼光
有兩三個甚至刻意避開
最難過是我大個子的鄰居約翰
隔着籬笆問我：
你真的沒有問題？
問了兩次，還禁止他的女兒
到我家和小文一起做功課
原來世衛的專家說：
只有不健康的人才需要戴口罩
我戴了，不是有病麼？
但健康不健康
誰知道呢，可以像圖靈那樣測謊？
詭異的東西，往往不露徵象
病了，是否就道德有虧？
我除了口罩才敢到教堂
彷彿這是瀆神的舉動
所以，我也不去了
弟弟，不要再把妖物寄來
我一直想一如其他人那樣生活
我最怕敵意的眼光

Letter from Canada

Brother, don't send me these masks anymore

I wore one for a stroll in the park

Everyone threw me odd looks, clearly bothered

A handful walked away altogether

The worst was John, our neighbour, the big guy

asked me across the garden fence from his side:

Are you really alright?

He asked me twice, and banned his daughter

from doing homework with our Samantha

It turned out that experts at WHO said:

Mask is only for the sick

Was I sick, if I wore a mask?

But healthy or sick

Who'd know? Could it, like in Turing's polygraph, be exposed?

These secretive things had no symptoms, no signs

Was it some form of moral deficiency, if I were sick?

I had to take the mask off when I went to church

as though it were some kind of blasphemy

I stopped going finally

Don't send me these evil masks anymore, Brother

My only wish is to live like everybody else

Not under watchful, hostile eyes

愛情真詭異

今春愛情真詭異
但聽它喟喟低啐一兩聲
愛理不理的
不夠熱情
只是有點發燒
許是一見鍾情吧
還不能肯定
它是陰性

才不過十四天
它忽爾爆發激情
太激烈了，繾綣纏綿
難捨難離，要生要死
連自己也吃不消
它宣佈出櫃
原來是陽性

Love can be weird

Love is really weird this spring
I heard it mutter and complain
A little distant
A little cold
And a slight fever it runs

It's love at first sight conceivably
Nothing definitive
It is surely negative

Fourteen days it has been
and passion suddenly erupts
Too vehemently intense
this inseparable, life or death romance
Even love itself can't take it anymore
So from the closet it emerges
It is positive after all

瘟疫與將軍

當疫情逐漸失禁
（不是失控，用字要準確）
將軍下令要用飛彈向病毒攻打
三天內倘瘟疫還不肯乖乖投降
（馬上計時，倒數七十二小時）
將軍打過好幾場仗
都很漂亮，你不見
他左右襟上掛滿了勳章
對上一場，攻破了不能攻破的
黑洞海洋
士卒一無損傷
更深入敵陣
對手呢，無法估算
全數陣亡
各位手足，將軍說
（他很親切，毫無架子
簡直可以和我們一起吃火鍋）
我們要抱必勝的決心
美帝電影甚麼的「嘔壁」
（Outbreak，將軍帶點動聽的口音）
不是把疫城一股腦兒炸個稀巴爛
難道我們炸彈的威力比不上？
這電影在軍營裏播了又播
只播上半場，我們都會背了
當疫城灰飛煙滅

大家拍手叫好的時候
小D開始忐忑不安
瘟疫以來，他就患上憂鬱症
阿彌陀佛，他希望要炸的地方
他的親朋戚友並不在場

The Pandemic and the General

When the pandemic became incontinent
(not insuppressible, we had to be factual)
The General ordered missiles to be launched
if the virus refused to surrender within 3 days
(counting down 72 hours straight away)
The General had won many battles
all with pluck and pomp. Didn't you see
both his breast plates full of medals?
In the last battle, he conquered the insurmountable
Black Hole
Not a single of our soldiers lost
deep behind enemy lines
The opponents, casualty beyond count
all perished at the frontline
"Fellow comrades," addressed the General
(Such a nice man he was, no pretension
We could practically share a hot-pot)
"To win this war we need determination
This 'owlback' whatever American movie"

(Outbreak, pronounced in the General's pleasant twang)
"Wasn't the infected town blown to teeny-weeny bits?
Isn't our artillery as powerful in a blitz?"
In the barracks, that movie was played again and again
We knew the rest by heart as it began
When the infected city was bombed into oblivion
and everyone cheered in triumph
Little D became distressed
Since the pandemic he had been depressed
Hail Mary, Mother of God, he prayed with fervour
that his folks were never near the area

Translator's note:
Hot pot – also known as steamboat. One of the first group infections in Hong Kong involved a hot pot dinner gathering.

瘟疫與煙民

他跑到辦公室外
把口罩扯到顎下
點火，大力抽了一下煙
他從事保險行業
鎮日對着熒屏工作
網上的訊息他一概不信
因為沒有所云fact-check
一位網民說抽煙可以殺菌
這個，他信了
他告訴一直要他戒煙的老婆
這，經過他多年的人身測試
所有病毒的研究
就是遺漏了煙民與非煙民
確診染病的比例
或者，他點燃另一根煙
說：已經做了研究
世衛那個埃塞俄比亞的頭頭
由於不好鼓勵
隱瞞了答案

Pandemic and Smokers

To the outside of the office he made a sprint
He pulled the face mask down to his chin

Cigarette lit, a deep drag he seized

He was an insurance agent

Sat all day in front of a computer station

He did not believe anything online

None of it had been *fact-checked*

A fellow netizen said smoking killed germs

This, though, he believed

To his wife who pestered him to quit, he affirmed

from many years of personal experimentation

None of the virus research out there

studied the infection correlation

between smokers and non-smokers

Or, lighting another cigarette, he alleged:

Such clinical studies had indeed been done

but the W.H.O. Ethiopian head

had pulled a fast one

and concealed the answers from everyone

瘟疫和花花

花花是隻普通的貓
不過更高傲，更霸道
鄰家的大狗也怕牠
死開，牠大姊咆哮，保持安全距離
我昨天殺死三隻蠹魚
兩隻蟑螂
今天還沒有發市
你們平日不是奴才那樣
戴了皮口罩？
不停污染街道
早晚散播病毒？
鎮日坐嬰車、要抱抱
再不會走路
難得有一點日照
看我到屋外散開碎步
豎起葵扇似的尾巴
喵喵，沒有在動物之間大流行
你以為是政府的功勞？
萬一我也受了你們的傳染
我也是全球受感染的第一貓

Pandemic and Fa-fa

Fa-fa is just an ordinary cat
but for her haughtiness, her aggressiveness
The big dog next door keeps its distance
Get lost, she roared, keep a safe distance
I slayed three silverfish yesterday
and two roaches
I have yet to make a killing today
Aren't you all minions with your slavish nuzzle,
under your pathetic leather muzzle?
Soiling the streets and sidewalks
spreading germs all day and night?
All day, you sit in a pram begging for hugs
No longer able to walk
Now, in this rare bit of sunlight
watch me take a leisurely stroll out of the house
like fan palm the tail outspread
Miao, you think it's the government's credit
the virus hasn't spread in the animal world?
If I end up infected by you people
I would be the world's first coronavirus feline

瘟疫與狗

早上遛狗的時候
街上空寂無人
店鋪全關閉了
我彷彿走進科幻電影
的末世，化武戰爭之後
我的小狗是個守在門口
對外人兇囂的殺手
一旦開門，就夾着尾巴竄逃
牠在家裏隔離了十四天
搞得全屋臭氣熏天
如今出外放風
既雀躍，又畏怯
牠拖着我走在前頭
可左右張望提防
你知道，只有回家的狗
視歸如死，在後頭跟你角力
忽然，路旁轉出一隻大狗
拖着後面跟蹌一位大姐
大狗發現小狗，馬上衝過來
小狗，我的媽
怕的撲上我的身上
手腳都在發抖
那位大姐死命牽扯着大狗
轉頭，一個在咆哮
另一個，留下蔑視的眼神

走了

「你怕甚麼，難道牠會吃了你？」
「誰說我怕牠，你沒注意麼？」
「注意甚麼？」
「牠沒戴口罩。」
「你呢？」
「但我斷定那大姐來自廣西玉林，那頭狗，哼，」
「怎麼啦？」
「死定了，捱過瘟疫，也捱不過六月的吃狗節。」

Pandemic and Dogs

In the morning when I walked the dog
there was no one around
The shops were all closed down
I might have walked into a sci-fi film set
an apocalyptic world wrecked by biological warheads
My little dog would be the vicious killer
guarding the door from whoever wanted to enter
Once the door opened, fleeing with tail between his legs
My dog had been quarantined for a fortnight
A stinking mess it had made of the house
When it was let out finally
exulted, yet intimidated
in a frenzy of delight, it charged ahead, me behind
still fearful, watchful, it warily looked around

Dogs see home as worse than death, you know
and fight tooth and nail to stay out
Suddenly, a big dog appeared on the road
Behind its tail a woman stumbled
The big dog saw my small dog, and stormed at once
My small dog, my goodness
jumped onto me in great terror
shaking all over
The woman held the big dog back with all her might
They turned, one of them was growling
The other cast a contemptuous look
and walked away

"Why the hell are you so scared? Was it going to eat you alive?"
"Who said I was afraid? Didn't you notice?"
"What?"
"It had no mask on."
"What about you?"
"But the woman was from Yulin, Guangxi, I am sure.
That dog of hers…"
"What about it?"
"Dead meat! It may survive the epidemic,
but surely not the June Yulin Dog Meat Festival."

瘟疫與老闆

分公司的經理在電郵安排
彈性上班的時間：
員工在家工作
每周兩天上班
提供一個口罩
保護衣兩人輪替穿著
裝備已確保一個月的存貨
搓手液不缺
但洗手會更安全
洗手吧，不用顧慮水費
倘有意見，積極的
請直接告訴我
三分二人離職之後
業務逐漸改善
收支平衡
全賴領導有方
董事長當我們是子弟那樣訓誡
當我們是子女那樣愛護
我感到無比的幸福
看着董事長掛在公司的尊容
誰不眼泛淚光？
我希望留下的員工跟我一樣
謹守崗位，努力工作
為了報答，自動減薪

董事長正在抽着雪茄
在另一個屏幕無意中看到
自己尊容的倒影
有點尷尬，然而
自忖心理正常
別人的好意豈能拒絕
對其他同事也是正能量
艱難時期，正正不要製造恐慌
在電腦上按了一個讚
心想：人材難得
非要留住不可
總經理放完無薪假期
合該由他接班

The Pandemic and the Boss

The Branch Manager announced on email
the new flexi-time schedule:
All staff will work from home
with 2 days a week at the office
One mask will be provided
One PPE between 2 colleagues alternated
There will be ample supply to last a month
Also, there is no shortage of hand sanitizer
but nothing beats soap and water
Go ahead, wash hands, don't worry about the water bill
Any opinion, constructive ones

let me know at once
Two third of our staff are now gone
The business is gradually improving
We have now achieved break-even
Thanks to the Management
The Managing Director talks to us like his children
and looks after us like his offspring
This sense of joy I feel is overwhelming
Look up at the MD's portrait in the office
Who can hold back happy tears?
I hope every employee who remains, like me,
will do the utmost, work the hardest
and, as a token of appreciation, take a pay cut

The Managing Director, cigar in his mouth
caught from another monitor
his very own reflection
A little embarrassed he felt, nevertheless
he considered himself levelheaded
and could not refuse an act of kindness
It was also a positive email for the company
No reason to cause panic at times of great difficulty
Give it a Like, he did
He reckoned: Good people are difficult to come by
We should do our best to keep this guy
The General Manager's post, whose incumbent is on furlough
is a job the Branch Manager can take over

瘟疫與南北國

南方國忽爾瘟疫暴發
源頭遍查不獲
人傳人，狗傳貓
下流傳上流
傳到了軍方
數月後全國失控
對北方國
不戰而降

北方領袖躊躇滿志，說：
還不容易麼，只派了兩個特工
轉飛兩地，就到了沒有封關的南方
他們沒帶武器
不發燒，沒徵兆
不過，哈哈，身染劇毒
一個進了教會
另一個，去看球賽

Pandemic North and South

In Country South, a pandemic suddenly flared
from a virus of source unknown
From folks to folks, cats to dogs,
lower to upper class it travelled

Then it reached the military
Chaos within months across the country
To Country North, at once
the South capitulated without a punch

In Country North, the leader smugly said:
A piece of cake; two agents were all it takes
to fly around, through the border of the South they entered
No weapons were required
No symptoms, no fever
O well, ha-ha, armed with a deadly virus
one entered a church
the other a soccer match

瘟疫與偵探

你要找出事件的真相
告訴你，別害你自己
已經有四個探員，斃了
一個上班時汽車轟掉
兩個再不敢坐車
就死在路邊
一個，手機莫名其妙地觸電
你回到兇案現場
證據都沒有了，沒有
指紋、兇器、血漬
全都抹得乾淨
溫馨警示，你想成為第五個？
你看得太多偵探電影
完場前總是正邪對決
揭穿了整個警署與黑幫勾結
伸張了甚麼的正義
這是好萊塢傳來的瘟疫
你要追尋真相，很好
可甚麼是真相呢？
我們有最先進的監控
測謊機，識別靈長類的面相
但也並不依賴機械
還得配合人手操作
世情那麼複雜
豈能那麼單純

獨力對抗
你說你受得了
可你的親朋戚友也受得了麼？
有一晚，風高月黑
你會被逮捕
你的家裏搜出毒品、贓款
你成為了最大的兇嫌

Pandemic and Detectives

The truth you have to find out

And, let me tell you, watch out

Four detectives are already dead

One shot in his car on the way to work

Two others too scared to take their vehicles

but still killed on the road

and the last electrocuted by his own cell phone

You'd return to the crime scenes

No more evidence, no more

prints, weapons, blood stains

All wiped clean

Gentle reminder: don't be the fifth

You watched too many cop movies

They all ended with battles between good and evil

exposés of police and gang collusion

A return to justice, of sorts

But this is a pandemic, from Hollywood it spread

You want the truth. Fine.

But what's the truth?

We have the most advanced surveillance

lie detection, primate facial recognition

But we cannot rely on automation

We also need human intervention

The world is complex

The solution can't be simple

To fight it on your own

you said you could

But could your friends and family do that too?

One of these nights, dark and moonless

you will be arrested

From your home, drugs and money found and collected

You will become the prime suspect

病者

我看見它留下的指紋
在森林，在曠野
我看見它
在黝黑無人的地方
攀爬跳躍
雙眼靈靈閃光
我看見它倒弔着睡覺
把這顛倒了的世界
顛倒過來
我看見它凝神聆聽
大自然的音樂
我看見它
愉快地飛翔
然後看見它老大不願意
走進喧鬧的菜市場
隨饕餮們大吃大喝
我沒有參加他們的狂歡節
反而跟他們一樣
成為了病號
住進了隔離的疫房
所有人對我害怕、厭惡
看見我的人都穿戴保護
我甚麼都再看不見了
最後，成為了一個鬼祟的
數字，一縷輕煙

The Sick

I see the fingerprints it left behind
in the forest, in the wild
I see it
in dark, uninhabited land
crawling and juggling
eyes aglow with piercing slant
I see it sleeping upside down
turning this downside-up world
round and round
I see it listen attentively
to the singing of the wild
I see it
take wing gleefully
Then with much much dragging of its feet
enter the hustle-bustle veg-market reluctantly
and, next to the connoisseurs, binge in abandon
I am not a part of their merriment
But like them I become
a statistic of the sick
To the isolation ward I'm relegated
Feared and detested
Met only by people in protective clothing
I no longer see anything
but me turning, in the end, into an obscure
number, going up in smoke.

和病毒的距離

在狹窄的通道上
一百米外這個陌生人迎面而來
他看來矮小瘦削
頭髮蓬鬆
皮膚黝黑
肯定不是我的同類
五十米了，我必須當機立斷
是側身閃過，還是轉頭
急步離開
這豈不是歧視？
賸下五米了
他一連咳嗽了兩下
我噗噗心跳
我要窒息了

這個人沒有戴口罩

A deadly distance

In the narrow passageway

A stranger approaches from a hundred meters

He looks small and frail

Hair tousled

Skin sallow

Definitely not my kind
50 more meters. I have to decide
to turn around or squeeze
past by his side
Does this count as discrimination?
Five meters now
He coughs in quick succession
My heart skips
I cannot breathe

This man has no mask on

王子的故事

王子剛到達古堡
被醫護人員截停了
他很不爽
在他自己的地方
他檢測是陽性
但沒有病徵，沒有
當然就非常健康
他是全國首富
乘坐私人飛機
四五千人送行
他和每一個人握手
親吻女孩子的面頰
報道說她們都很傷心
他轉乘飛快的宇宙之星
再坐上特大大的轎車
同時坐得下五十個保鑣
兩個財政部長、四個銀行大班
八個御醫，六十四個供奉
據說，他那位拒絕離世的祖父
也一直坐在車裏
一座流動的行宮
其間他路過皇宮六十星飯店
大宴隨行官員
即捕即吃了野生牛扒
還吃了水裏的，會飛的甚麼

不便説了，王子不喜歡炫富

只喝了埃塞俄比亞咖啡

兩杯羅馬馬亞卓古拉紅酒

抽了兩口古巴巴雪茄

在更衣室裏

整理一下儀容

戴上義髮，並不假

一個隨從説「假髮」

被他問了責

他謝了頂，可誰知道呢

他只知道，門外有大批記者

他約會了古堡的異國公主

事先張揚會向她求婚

只要她同意

就會把整個古堡整個城市

買下，修橋搭路

保證全城工人有飯下肚

古堡會變新堡

她不可能不同意啊

他對着麥克風狂笑

接連大聲咳嗽

因為一個記者很幽默

問他可是又到古堡捉鬼了？

這個記者，要嗎成為頭條

要嗎，從此只專責分派報紙

豈知，在古堡前

忽爾大霧瀰漫

正想抓牢從天垂下

搖晃不定的長髮
卻被溫馨地勸止了
理由是全城九成多的人受了感染
開始發燒、胸痛、乏力
他自己呢，看來像喪屍
不過都無需進入隔離營，因為
沒有一個營裝得下所有的病人
他的如意算盤打亂了
四個銀行家死了三個
賸下的一個，要兩個呼吸機幫助
唯有在城的四周築起圍牆
御醫都換上了防彈衣
跟一種神出鬼沒的敵人作戰
據說幸得不死，六成人吧
自會調適，產生抗體
很簡單，首席御醫說
病毒也需要宿主，而這
完全是王子管理哲學的複製
你只能欺壓、奴役
可不能把全部人打殺
不然，還誰來聽你使喚？
你豈不變成沒有人民的國王？
為免兩敗俱傷
在一個絕不晴朗的日子
王子和瘟疫交換和平合約
互吻對方
那賸下的六成人無不雀躍頌讚
但有一個女子以長髮為繩

偷偷溜出了城外
溜出了沒厘頭的
故事之外

Ballad of the Prince

The Prince arrived at the castle
He was intercepted by the medics
None too pleased with the hassle
happened in his own land too
His test result was positive
Without symptoms, without signs
he was nothing but healthy and fine
As the richest man in the nation
he travelled on private aviation
Thousands bid him farewell
He shook hands with them as well
and planted a kiss on every girl's cheek
The girls were all broken-hearted, thus reported
He changed to board the light-speed Universe's Star
Followed by the limousine of XL-sized car
accommodating at once 50 bodyguards
two finance ministers, four bankers
eight imperial physicians and 64 valets
And this ancestor of his who refused to die
was rumoured to also reside
in this limousine - the mobile palace

On the way, he passed by a royal 60-star resort

Wined and dined his entourage and court

with game steak from freshly hunted wildlife

with delicacies from the sky and the sea

No need for specifics; the Prince was very low-key

He had only a cuppa Ethic-nopian Koffee

a few glasses of Chateau Dracula Burn-undy

and a puff or two of Cuban Ban-cigars

Inside his dressing chamber

he finetuned his appearance

Put on a hair piece – mind you – not a wig

An attendant said something resembling "fake"

and was made accountable

The Prince had gone bald, but who would know

For now, he knew reporters had gathered outside the castle

An appointment had been made with the Princess of this foreign
   stronghold

in advance, he announced, to offer her a marriage proposal

Should she agree to his proposal

he would buy, together with the city, the entire castle

Major expenditure on infrastructure

to keep the whole city fed and happy

Ancient castle would become brand-new castle

She could not but accept the proposal

In front of the microphone he laughed in glee

followed by a spate of coughing

because a reporter was being funny

and asked if he intended, in the castle, to do some ghost-busting?

This reporter would either become himself a news headline

or forever the newspaper delivery guy

Suddenly, around the castle

Dense fog arose

The Prince, about to grab hold

of the dangling long hair from above

was advised gently not to do so

For over 90 percent of the populace were infected

Fever, chest pain, fatigue, you named it

The Prince himself looked like a walking dead

But there was still no need for quarantine, because

no camp was large enough for the number of patients

His fancy plan was thrown into confusion

Three out of four bankers were dead

The one remaining struggled on two respirators

The only way was to lock-down the city with high walls

Fit out the court physicians in combat gear

to fight enemies as ghostly as spectres, he feared

Rumours had it that those, about 60 percent, who were spared

developed antibodies in their systems

Simply put, the Chief Royal Medical Officer declared

Antigens needed a host, an exact replication

of your Royal Highness's administration

You could suppress and enslave

But the subjects you couldn't all eradicate

or, there would be no one left to dictate

Would you rather become a king with no subject?

To avoid more bloodshed

On a day far from perfect

The Prince and the Pandemic exchanged a peace treaty

Sealed with a kiss from both parties

The surviving 60 percent, jubilant, was all approving

But a woman, on rope made with long hair trailing

Stole past the city enclosure

and exited the nonsensical

fairytale

空椅

十四張空椅
一月的時候

二十四張，三月二十九日
宣佈了限聚令

午飯，我點了咖喱牛腩
以為薑黃素可以抗疫
這是阿文打聽回來的
但他後來一邊為椅子消毒
一邊悄悄告訴我：必須地道
我幾乎吃的是全包宴
全飯堂只有我
和另外一個
他距離我
何止一點五米
簡直是長江黃河

阿文呢？我問
隔離去了
他的樓宇有人感染
十四天後復工？
問得好，你不是數過麼
全店二十六張椅子
沒有一張不在守待

盼望離去的會回來
減了一點租
還不夠給人工
能否撐得住，誰知道

Empty chairs

14 empty chairs
in January

24 chairs, March 29th
Prohibition of Gathering declared

For lunch, I ordered brisket curry
assuming the turmeric could fight the virus
something Ah Man told me before
But later Ah Man quietly amended
while disinfecting the chairs: it depends
I almost had the whole restaurant to myself
In the dining hall, it was just me
and another person
who kept a distance
of much more than 1.5 meters in measurement
I'd say as much as the Yangtze and the Yellow rivers put together

Where's Ah Man? I asked
Quarantined

Someone in his building tested positive
Will he return in 14 days?
Good question. You counted them before
those chairs, all 26 of them
Every single one of them longing
for the return of those who left
The little rental rebate
hardly covers salary outlay
Can we stay open, who knows?

報告瘟疫期間的生活

老師要我們報告瘟疫期間的生活
我回覆說：一直努力讀書
做運動，也幫手做做家務
偶然也跟媽媽到超市
拎一籃子油鹽廁紙公仔麵
一次，我下街時忘了戴口罩
我伸直頭顱讓店門口的小姐探熱
她拒絕了，我埋怨媽媽沒有提醒我
原來她顧着和鄰居交談
說這是親子活動
此外，我每隔半小時就洗手
我並且連腳也洗了
我真有點懷念學校
盼望快些可以復課
我這樣寫了老師預期的答案
老師給我兩個讚，還說瘟疫令人改變
我取得了這學年最高的分數
她平日老是兇巴巴的瞪着我
所以我喜歡瘟疫
三個月來，不用回校上課的日子
我不停打機，上網
翻看朗拿甸奴、美斯的球賽
重溫十多齣《復仇者聯盟》
白癡才悶得發慌

Report on Life during the Pandemic

The teacher asked us to report on our lives during the pandemic

My response: I had been studying

exercising, helping with household chores

and occasionally shopping with my mum at the stores

carrying groceries: oil, salt, toilet rolls, instant noodles and more

Once, I forgot my face mask when I was out shopping

I stuck my head out to the shop lady for temperature-taking

She refused; I blamed my mum for not having reminded me

she was busy chatting with the neighbour next door

telling her what a family activity shopping was

In addition, I washed hands every half an hour

Even my feet were washed too

I really missed going to classes

I hope schools will soon be open to us

I thus wrote what the teacher expected me to report

She gave me two Excellent and declared pandemic reformed people

I received the highest mark of the entire school year

The teacher normally gave me her most severe glare

I love the pandemic

For the three months when I have had no school

I could play computer games all the way through

or watch online matches of Ronaldinho and Messi

or the dozen movies of "The Avengers" series

Bored? Only idiots get bored!

不見得完全被討厭

我不受歡迎，卻又不見得完全被討厭
恨和愛，誰都知道，往往交纏
要是讓我參加普選
怕甚麼呢，跨媒體，越國界
野生動物也未必不投我一票
我從大自然裏來
也可以棲身水渠、茅廁
和廢青、暴民打成一片
我可以參加狂歡節
參加同鄉會的團拜
參加戲子的拍攝
加入他們的爭風，或者爭辯
我喜歡二氯苯乙酮的氣味
胡椒噴霧令我食慾大振
當我成為宗教
用各種語言禱告
就可以零團費，無需簽證
免費坐車，乘飛機
到處自由參觀
倦了就睡進醫護人員的保護衣裏
他們每天工作十四小時
最危險的地方最安全
我確信，相處日久
終會說服皂液、酒精
改變它們的敵視

它們本來就沒有強大的意志
只需調整一下成分
而且，以為洗手洗到皮膚皸裂
就可以把仇恨洗去？
以為戴上口罩
就可以逃避追捕？
這是原罪
讓我們重新學習
人類的腦袋曾經無意中刪去
這麼的一種愛

Not entirely disliked

I am not popular, but I'm not necessarily entirely disliked

Love and hate, as everyone knows, are often entangled

If I were to run in a general election

I'm afraid - across all media, span over borders -

wild animals may not necessarily deny me a vote

From mother nature I emerge

In gutters and outhouses, I immerse

I can mix with hopeless youths and violent mobs

I can join in festivities

or celebrations of any clan associations

or be one of the crew among actors

to bicker for fame and fight for favours

I love the scent of chloroacetophenone

Pepper spray gives me an appetite boost

Once I become their religion
and people pray to me in different languages
I can travel the world
at zero cost, with no entry visa
free transport, free flights
sleep in PPE suit of doctors and nurses when I am tired
They work 14 hours a day
The most dangerous domain is also the safest place
I firmly believe, given time
I will convince soap and alcohol some day
to give up their animosity
They are not the strong-willed kind
It only takes some tweaking to change their mind
Anyway, what makes you think washing hands till the skin cracks
will wash hatred away?
And donning a mask will allow you to
keep pursuers at bay?
This is the original sin
Let us learn again
- from human brains it was inadvertently removed -
this kind of love

扔棄的口罩

一個口罩躺在泥污的地上
沒有去到它應該去的地方
它曾受盡愛寵，高價爭取
為了保護某一張臉
漂亮的，普通的
老的，少的
懸掛在耳朵的兩邊
撐起整個屏障
按壓上部的金屬片
溫柔地，要它緊貼
自己的鼻樑
再輕拉下緣，彼此調整
適應，相濡以沫
這一刻，這一張臉
是多麼真誠
付託了整個生命
它感動得想哭
然而，彷彿一夜的激情
過後，命定分手
但扯下來就走
一句好話也沒有
它被扔棄了，而且
隨手就扔棄在路邊

有些人，某一張臉
就是這樣對待愛情

Mask discarded

A mask laid on the dirt ground
It didn't go to where it should be
Once it was much cherished, in high demand
to protect certain faces
Comely faces, homely faces
Faces old or young
Hooked onto the side of the ears
from which the entire barrier is mounted
The metal strip on top is pressed
gently, snugly contoured
to hug tightly the ridge of the nose
Then softly the bottom is tugged
adjusted, in each other's embrace
At this moment, the face
in all earnestness, true thankfulness
to the mask, its entire being entrusted
is moved beyond tears
Yet, a passionate night now over
the relationship destined to be severed
Ripped out, ditched
without a kind word
discarded off-hand
It is now abandoned by the roadside

Some people, some faces
treat love this way

這是我熟悉的城市麼？

這是我熟悉的城市嗎？
每年初夏我回來
站在同一碼頭同一的支柱上
我的確有點戀舊
風急，一片灰濛濛
的水氣，人稀少了
只一兩個坐在椅上
老遠地分隔開
沉默，失神地看海
也有一兩個在垂釣
都戴上了口罩
我認不出誰
抑或他們忽然老去
晚上更寧靜得出奇
不見遊船河的旅行團
吵鬧，喧嘩
拎着大大小小冒牌的土產

這還是我熟悉的地方？
十幾年前，禽流感肆虐
全球死了八百多人
鳥類，本來不少已瀕危
可沒有人會統計
彷彿都帶來病毒
為了自救，我們成立流感紀念館

流動的，在空中
從一隻鳥傳到另一隻鳥
一個窩，到另一個窩
記憶短暫，所以
世世代代要牢牢記取
因為我們曾經受害
那時我還遠未出世啊
然後，十七年前非典肺炎
人類死亡過千
想來荒謬，自詡聰明的人類
妄想病毒可以打敗
他們懂得咬文嚼字
紀錄一大堆
就是不曾老實面對
難道真要我們飛翔的堂兄弟
進入饕餮的肚皮
才能喚醒沉痛的感官？
人類的記憶原來比鳥還要短暫
瘟疫又來了
這地方，還是我認識的麼？

半年前，我遇到一隻黑臉琵鷺
告誡我不要再回來
泥灘濕地正在不斷撤退
這裏的空氣
瀰漫西埃斯、二氯甲烷
令生靈火燒似的灼痛
咳嗽、嘔吐，還喪失視力

不停流淚，可不由於失望、憤懣
黑臉說，無數同類中毒
牠是倖存的一個
這地方，又不是你的故鄉
你會在一棵倒塌的樹築巢麼？
你何不流浪，像歌曲
流浪，到遠方？

但我為甚麼要流浪
到一個我沒有記憶的地方？
我到過南北的大江大河
記得我飛過大小磨刀的水域時
認識了兩條美麗的白海豚
今年流連水面，再沒有遇見
年輕時聽長輩說
塞納河、威尼斯、巴塞隆拿
會飛翔的，一生總要去一次
可如今整個歐美都淪為大疫區
死亡的數字遞增
屏幕上我看到一幕
美國人在荒島上挖掘
黯黑，長長的深坑
把失救的人掩埋
這不是歷史上的黑死病麼？
這，還是我認識的世界？

Is this the city I once knew?

Is this the city I once knew?
Every summer I return
and perch on the same post at the same pier
I am indeed the nostalgic kind
Wind rushes, a sky of grayish
water vapours, a few people
scattered on the benches
separated by distance
in silence, gazing at the ocean
A few of them are fishing
under their face masks
I don't recognize anyone
or they may have aged all of a sudden
The evening is incredibly serene
Tour groups on cruises are no longer seen
Those cantankerous, boisterous
laden-with-counterfeit-souvenir bunch

Is it still the place I once knew?
The place a dozen years before by Bird Flu ravaged
when worldwide, eight hundred people perished
Birds, some already on the brink of extinction
- no census enumeration -
were virus-carriers, it seemed
For self-protection, we set up influenza memorial centres
mobile, up in the air

from one bird to another

one nest to the next

Memories are short; please, future generations,

don't ever forget

that we were once victims

long before my time

Then, SARS that took place 17 years ago

killed humans in the thousands

Ridiculous it may now seem, people, self-conceited

harboured the delusion that the virus could be defeated

People are good with words

and keeping annals and chronicles

but not with facing facts

Do they really need our winged cousins

to enter their gluttonous stomachs

again, before they recall the pain?

People's memory is short, shorter than birds'

The pandemic is upon us again

This place, is it still the same one I knew?

Half a year back, I met a black-faced spoonbill

who warned me from returning

Mudflats, wetland, fast receding

The air, here,

was filled with CS and dichloromethane

searing burning pain on all living things

Choking, vomiting, loss of vision

Crying non-stop not just out of anger and frustration

Black-faced told me many birds were poisoned

He was lucky to have survived

It's not like this place is your hometown

Will you build a nest on a fallen tree?

Why not wander, like the song*

Wandering faraway?

But why should I wander away

to a place my memories do not hold sway?

I have flown past rivers in the north and south

I flew past the Brothers Islands before, I recalled,

meeting two beautiful White Dolphins

This year, I flew by, they were no longer there

When I was younger, birds that were older

would talk of Venice, Barcelona and the Seines

Places, for anyone who flies, to visit at least once in life

But now the whole western world has fallen prey to the virus

Death tolls mounting

On a screen I caught sight of a scene

On a remote island the Americans are digging

long, dark pits in the ground

to bury the deceased

Isn't it the same as the plague in history?

Is it, still, the world I once knew?

Translator's note:
The song mentioned in the original is called Olive Tree（橄欖樹）. The lyric was written by Sanmao (1943-1991), a writer/translator famous in the 80's in the Chinese speaking communities.

好社會的瘟疫

他斷定：他們是好社會的瘟疫
無藥可救
和一種病毒協商
太花時間
也太危險，不如
斃了

他發現自己同時
失去免疫力
那麼一陣微風細雨
他就感冒
作嘔，發燒，全身劇痛
死了

Pandemic of a good society

He concluded: they are the virus of a good society
There was no cure
Haggling with the virus
was too time consuming
and too dangerous. Might as well
die

He found out at the same time, for himself

there was no immunity

Exposure to a slight breeze and a bit of a drizzle

gave him the Flu

Vomit, fever, aching all over, he

died

瘟疫巨星

老師在視象裏說瘟疫也可以誕生偉人
他問：如果樹上的蘋果落到你的頭上？

——我會每天守在這樹下，一日一蘋果。
——我會反問：一個蘋果，還是許多個？
是甚麼原故，地震？危險；熟爛了？

老師：你們不會想深一層？

——真的落到頭上？我想我會暈了。
——偏偏選中我？我會懷疑這是文仔搞的鬼。
——有人把香蕉扔向卡路士[1]，因此發明香蕉射球[2]；
我呢，我會研究蘋果救球[3]。

老師：他是牛頓，他發現萬有引力。
視象裏出現牛頓像。

——萬有魅力？好長的鬈髮，他肯定是瘟疫巨星哦。

老師：我是說引力。

——cool！即是吸引人的魅力。

1　卡路士：羅拔圖‧卡路士（Roberto Carlos），巴西著名黑人球員；比賽時
　　有對方觀眾向他扔香蕉。
2　香蕉射球：Banana shot
3　蘋果救球：Apple save（此詞是我的創作）

Pandemic Superstar

Teacher said on Zoom that pandemic could give rise to great people
He asked: If apples fall onto your head from a tree...?

— I will stay everyday under the tree. An apple a day
— I will ask: One apple or many more?
Why, earthquake? Could be unsafe; maybe rotten?

Teacher: Think deeper, would you?

— Will it really hit my head? I am sure I will collapse.
— Why me? I will suspect it is Ah Man's foul play, perhaps.
— A banana thrown at Carlos inspired the Banana Shot
    Me, I will make the Apple Save* my next big shot

Teacher: I meant Newton who discovered Gravity, the force of
    attraction.
A video image of Newton emerged.

—Attraction? What long curly hair! He must be a pandemic superstar.

Teacher: I am talking about gravitational force that attracts everything.

—Cool! This superstar attracts everything.

Translator's note:
Apple Save is a coinage by the poet. It was inspired by Roberto Carlos "banana kick"
in 1997, one of the most impressive free kicks in football history. The treachery of
the ball was shaped like a banana.

在名店的廣場上踢球

疫情稍定，我和弟弟偷偷在名店的廣場上踢球
上次我不過抱着皮球走過
走過罷了，就被保安喝止
這不是小孩遊戲的地方
你老頭子賠得起麼？
現在好了，古馳、香奈兒、愛馬仕¹都關了門
像球會停止了比賽
保安，連工也保不住了
弟弟是巴塞，我是皇馬，我喜歡美斯²，但弟弟比我矮小
那我是誰呢，C朗³？我其實希望是麥巴比⁴
一次為了踢球逃學，被老師記了一次過
老師通知老爸，麥巴比？貴子弟真這樣當自己

可老爸告訴我一個逃獄大王的故事
他叫巴比龍⁵，不過是個小偷
卻被誣陷，囚禁到流放營裏
羈留的都是重犯，強姦，殺人
可沒有一個因為踢球
巴比龍，你知道嗎？即是蝴蝶
好球員，不是像穿花蝴蝶嗎？
蝴蝶怎耐得住禁錮
第一次越獄失敗，被收進禁閉室
黑暗，孤寂，會把人逼瘋
再次逃獄，被移送到孤懸高崖的惡魔島
外面是大大的大西洋

從沒有人可以逃出來
沒有人可以活着離開
但他沒有絕望
捱過了奴役、飢餓、疫症
得到難友的幫助，當然
也曾有人把他出賣
第三次，終於逃出了生天
我這古怪的老爸問：
你要自由，很好
但有這種不怕艱難，吃苦
沒有人比得上的意志麼？

我說不是沒得比，而是麥巴比
不是一樣麼，老爸忽然嚴肅起來：
溫布萊、伯納烏、諾坎普
九萬個觀眾的球場
通通封了；即在平時
哪一個球員不會受傷、生病？
不聽教練，不肯苦練
不守遊戲規矩，你以為
麥巴比還可以像蝴蝶
穿過重重的高牆
成為世上最佳的球員？

1　古馳：Gucci；香奈兒：Chanel；愛馬仕：Hermès
2　美斯：Messi
3　C朗：Cristiano Ronaldo
4　麥巴比：Mbappé
5　巴比龍：Papillon，意為「蝴蝶」，2017 年重拍電影，改編自真人的自傳。

Playing soccer in a luxury shopping plaza

The pandemic eases, snuck into the high-end plaza my brother and I
    played soccer

Last time I merely walked past with a ball

Just passing, a security guard bellowed

"This is no place for little fellows

Can your old man pay for any damages at all?"

Now, well, Gucci, Chanel, Hermès all closed their doors

like football clubs halted their games

This snob of a guard can't even guard his job

Little brother in Barça, me Real Madrid. I am a fan of Messi, but my
    brother is small

Who should I be, Ronaldo? I'd really like to be Mbappé

Once, I skived school to play football and received a demerit

Mbappé? The teacher called my Papa, that's who your son thinks he is

So Papa told me a tale about a prison break

Nicknamed Papillon; he was just a thief, a small-timer

Set up, framed, he was imprisoned and exiled

Along with rapists, murderers, all serious offenders

But none was there for football felonies

Papillon, do you know, was butterfly?

Great footballers, nimble like butterflies

could stand no imprisonment

The first escape attempt ended in isolation confinement

where darkness, loneliness would drive one mad

The next escape had him transferred to Devil's Island, perched on tall cliffs of giant proportion, surrounded by the Atlantic Ocean

No one escaped from this island

No one ever walked out alive

Yet he did not lose hope

Toils, hungers, diseases he endured

with help of fellow inmates. Of course

there were betrayals too

On the third attempt he regained freedom at last

My weirdo of a Papa asked:

You want freedom. Great

But do you have the same undaunted

inimitable will power?

I said I wanted to be Mbappé, the footballer; not a jailbreaker

It is all the same, Papa said, suddenly somber:

Wembley, Santiago Bernabeu, Camp Nou,

Stadiums for ninety thousand and more

All shut down; normally

setbacks, pains, illnesses are commonplace for any player

If he didn't listen to his coach, didn't work hard

didn't play by the rules of the game,

would Mbappé scale

the tallest hurdles like a butterfly

and become the best footballer in the world?

Translator notes:
Papillon, a 2017 movie remake by Michael Noer based on real life events.

最後的一場電影

我拉下門閘時街上已寂靜無人
最後的一場電影播完明天
電影院被禁令暫停
要停多久？只能扣問疫情
老闆說也好，不然
燈油火蠟，還有人工
小食部早已不做了
辭退了四個，另外兩個兼職
再另外兩個，近乎做義工
有時來，當新戲上演
有時不來，就沒人打掃
我負責票房，留守
這是區內最老的電影院
老何，老闆對我說
多年賓主，重開的時候
你回來，不過
要是找到更好的工作⋯⋯
他拍拍我的肩膊
忽爾提高嗓門：
老兵不死
我馬上浮現《鄧苟克大行動》的一幕
我答：繼續作戰
我最記得的其實是《鄧苟克戰役》
那是我童年時看過的一齣
我的夢想曾隨着電影飛翔

飛了好一陣，可飛不過大海洋

被炮火逐一擊落

但舊戲總有人翻拍，改編，再創造

這三個月，觀眾小貓三兩

急轉到最後的一場

只得一個和兩個

兩個顯然是情侶

坐下前，女的把椅子抹了又抹

脫下口罩，兩個頭就靠成一個頭

另一個，是常見的長者

坐到老遠，蓋上厚重的大衣

完場時要我把他喚醒

明天不要來了，我說

怎麼？明天結業？

不，我向他解釋

記得上一代老闆的口頭禪：

The show must go on

註：《鄧苟克大行動》（Dunkirk），2017 年，基斯杜化‧路蘭導演；《鄧苟克戰役》（Dunkirk），1958 年，萊斯利‧羅文（Leslie Norman）導演。

The Last Picture Show[1]

The streets were empty when I pulled the shutter

after the last picture tonight was finished

Tomorrow all cinemas will be banished

For how long? You'd better put the question to the virus

Why not, said the boss, or else

rent, rates, utilities and payroll keep coming

The snack bar was long gone

Four were let go, two were on furlough

The other two were paid like volunteers

showed up when there were new movies

didn't show up, then no cleaning duties

I looked after ticketing, holding the fort

of the oldest cinema in the vicinity

Ho, the boss said to me

You have worked here for so many years

Come back when we reopen, unless

you have found a better job…

A pat on the shoulder he gave me

And, suddenly, declared loudly:

Old Soldiers Never Die[2]

In my head a scene from *Dunkirk*[3] emerged

Together we fight on, I replied

What I remembered was the old *Dunkirk*[4]

I watched when I was a child

My dreams flying along with the motion pictures

for a long while, but never made it to the *wild blue yonder*[5]

before being gunned down one after another

But classics were never short of remakes, recasts and reboots

The past three months saw a clutch of moviegoers

At the last show tonight, there were

a couple and only one other customer

The couple were obviously an item

Before they settled, the girl wiped the seats over and over

Masks off, the two heads became one in tandem

The single person was the usual senior

seated well away from the screen under his thick coat

I woke him when the credits began to roll

Don't come tomorrow, I said

Why not? Out of business?

No, I offered

in the catch phrase of the old boss before last:

"The show must go on"

Translator's note:
1 The Last Picture Show – film directed by Peter Bogdanovich, 1971
2 An old army ballad: "Old soldiers never die, never die…they just fade away"
3 Dunkirk – remake directed by Christopher Nolan, 2017
4 'Old' Dunkirk – Film directed by Leslie Norman, 1958
5 The Wild Blue Yonder – directed by Werner Herzog, 2005

忘了

今早我找遍了找不到眼鏡原來一直掛在鼻樑上
從大廈出來馬上又要折返因為忘了戴口罩
我的呼吸不爽好像走出了太空艙
我醒來時竟忘了昨夜難得的夢
夢想我好像走過繁華璀璨忽然
落入一片荒漠朦朧
看見無數擱淺了的船隻
許多白色的骸骨
我揉揉眼睛，要自己保持清醒
慶幸親朋戚友在封城前
已移居去了金星
然後隨着人群擠進了超市
但忘了要買的是廁紙抑或公仔麵
末日到來，我到底還需要甚麼呢
我的氧氣只餘下二十分鐘
經過舊識的小店要不要站着吃一碗白果豆腐腦
那是我忘了的味道
我數不清我還忘了些甚麼
店主說好歹減了三個月租說着說着我發覺
我忘不了的是她美麗的笑容

Poor memory

The glasses I was searching for the entire morning were in fact wedged
   on the bridge of my nose
I left the building but I had to go back straight away for the face mask I'd
   forgotten
My breathing laboured as if I just stepped out from a spaceship
I woke up with no memory of the rare dream last night
In the dream, I seemed to walk through incredible riches
to descend, suddenly, onto mist-shrouded beaches
with numerous shipwrecks
white skeletons stranded
I rub my eyes, to stay awake
Happy that my folks have left town before the lockdown
to emigrate to Venus
Then into a packed supermarket I followed the crowd
But I forgot if I want toilet paper or instant noodles
Judgment day is nigh, what else will I require?
My oxygen would last another twenty minutes at most
Should I stand at the familiar shop on the way to eat a bowl of gingko
   tofu?
The taste of which I have forgotten
There were countless things I have forgotten, I could not keep tab
The owner was chatting away about the 3-month rent reduction and I
   realized
it was her beautiful smile I could not forget

生命就是這樣

探出頭來
掙開泥土的時候
那會是另一個世界
另一個春天
躲過了陰鬱的日子
你知道，只需要耐心
堅持；陽光會灑下金黃
再沾一些雨露
總可以活下來
活着就有希望
要活得比不好的東西長
生長，慢慢地茁壯
離開了的鳥兒
會回來，會的
會唱歌，雖然有時
嫌牠們太吵了，太張揚
帶來揮之不去的蟲蟻
鬼祟的病毒
有時，在歡愉裏
會忽爾憂來無方
就當是挑戰吧
必須好好地防備
春天會來而又去
再來的時候，會更擅變
更詭異，囂張

老套地說一句：
生命就是這樣
我想，你明白我的意思

That's life

When your head

emerges from the soil

you will find another world out there

Another spring

has survived the dull and dreary days

You know, with patience

persistence, the sun will cast its gold again

sprinkled with rain and dew

We will live

There will be hope if we still breathe

We will outlive harmful things

Grow, steadily stronger

Birds that have flown away

will return, and return, they will

with songs. Sometimes

they can be noisy, too rowdy

and bring with them obstinate insects

surreptitious germs

Sometimes, too, at the height of happiness

anxiety will strike

Let that be a reminder

to keep us on our toes

Spring comes and goes

It may return with more fickleness

More weirdness, more rudeness

As the saying goes,

C'est la vie

I am sure, you see

告訴你，我是因為瘟疫才活過來

告訴你，我是因為瘟疫才活過來
我走到海邊，那本來是一片污水
忽然也覺得它並非不好看
那些碎屑浮萍前後晃動
自有一種均衡的節奏
當船來了，變得激盪亢奮
之後，又修復過來
我開始聽到水鳥的說話
一隻說：沒有魚哦
另一隻說：忍耐一下吧
聲音悄悄，好像
不想別的人和魚聽到
我坐在碼頭的椅上
其他椅子，坐了疏落的長者
多天來，我總看到同一位在垂釣
可沒釣到甚麼
仍然那麼凝神專注
收拾離開時還吹着口哨
看海的人，我是最年輕的一個
傍晚了，陽光灑落
海面鍍上一層金黃
我脫下口罩
呼吸新鮮的空氣
活着真好
告訴你，我一直生無所戀

也無所爭取

明天，我要重新抓一份工作

Let me tell you, I'm alive again because of the pandemic

Let me tell you, I'm alive again because of the pandemic

I walked to the seashore, a stretch of murky water it was

Somehow it didn't look too uninviting

Those drifting bits of flotsam, undulating

in a rhythmic composition of their own

When a ship came near, they whirled and twirled in allegro

Then, they slowed and returned to normal

I could hear the shore birds, talking to each other

One muttered: There are no more fishes

Another whispered: Be patient

in a tiny voice, as if

to keep it from the fish, and the other people

I sat on a bench at the pier

A handful of old folks scattered on other benches

For days, I saw the same angler fishing

to no avail, nothing

Yet he was focused, dedicated

and left whistling when it was time to pack

Among the sea gazers, I turned out to be the youngest

Dusk came, the sea pane plated

in a layer of fine gold dust

I took my mask off

Took a deep breath of freshness

Amazing to be alive

Let me tell you, I had no one to live for

nothing to strive for, and likely

in vain if I try

But tomorrow, I will grab myself a new job

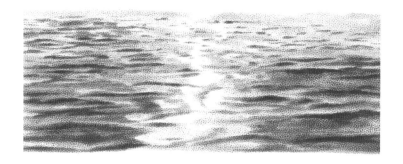

紅樓夢裏的瘟疫
——並仿脂批

躲在紅樓裏就可以做一百二十回

沒有瘟疫的夢（是外星的恐襲）

因為書本都經過消毒（這是紙抄本，網絡傳收則需防火牆）

我不戴口罩因為口罩是防止下人亂説話（是否我也要收口）

我也不洗手因為我沒有和壞人握手

我可以過一種諧和、牢靠的生活

重建一座頹敗的家園

重提忠孝節義，這是後續的命題

這也是我出生以來的追求（誰不嚮往呢，即使是虛擬）

我偶然看出窗外

我的窗都裝置了防彈玻璃

隔絕噪音、輻射、毒氣

窗框外，桂花、梅花盛開

還有叢叢芭蕉

可以經歷大暑嚴寒

可以詠菊，詠芙蓉

永不凋謝（果爾洋洋大觀）

且無勞打掃，避免污染

數不盡亭榭堂館，山石玲瓏

橋樑與迴廊，豈能走遍

還是遙遙觀看最好

早晨的時候會有鳥飛過（這之前倒較罕見）

只需按鈕，就可以聽到牠們唱歌

有七首可供選擇（是每天輪替？欠交代）

有一次我按錯了（活該）

聽到溫馨的提示：

別再按錯，你是否需要幫助？（客氣了）

我滿懷感激，自信可以多補一百二十回

讓十二金釵重聚

出家的回來

哭喊的日子過去，新添

無數任勞任怨的丫鬟

都是智能機械

不用錢一萬八千去買（都要嚴肅正經，別帶壞少主）

因為，我只需依時充電

複製若干舊有的詞彙

替換一些生鏽了的零件

譬如眼球、心肝（這最是關鍵）

The Pandemic Dream of the Red Chamber
——Annotation à la *Zhipi* [1]

Hiding in the Red Chamber, I can make 120 chapters [2]

of pandemic-free dreams (They are really terrorist attacks from outer space)

because books have all been sanitized (For prints only; digital copies
   require firewall)

I do not wear face masks because they are to prevent servants speaking
   nonsense (Should I keep my mouth shut too?)

I do not wash hands because I do not shake hands with bad persons

I can spend my life in harmonious, secured solace

rebuilding this once dilapidated place

reviving loyalty, filial piety, integrity and morality; but these quests can
  wait

they are lifelong pursuits of mine (Aren't they, even only virtual, everyone
  else's?)

I glance out of the windows

All the panes are bullet-proof glass

to stave off noises, radiation and poisonous gases

Beyond the windows, osmanthus and plum blossoms in the vista

and thicket upon thicket of trees of bananas

You can endure high heat and cold so bitter

You can sing to chrysanthemums, chant to hibiscus

that never ever wither (Indeed spectacular)

No need for cleaning, no decomposing

Countless pavilions, porticoes and intricate rock gardens

bridges, verandahs, too many to explore

It is better to visit from a distance

In the morning, birds fly by (They were rare before)

You press a button and they will sing for you

There are seven songs in the selection (A different one each day? Didn't say)

Once, I pressed the wrong button (Served me right)

And received a gentle reminder:

Please press the correct button; do you require assistance? (That was mild)

I am grateful and confident I could add another 120 chapters

Let the twelve Beauties of Jinling reunite

Let those who have forsaken the world return

The crying days now over, and all maids

replaced by hardworking, never-complaining

artificial-intelligence robots

No need to pay 18,000 copper yuan for each (They should be well-behaved

  lest they become bad influence to the young lords)

Because, all I need to do is recharge the battery periodically

duplicate certain old vocabulary

exchange some rusty parts

Like eyes and hearts (Those are the keys)

Translator's note:

1 Dream of the Red Chamber or Story of the Stone (紅樓夢) is a novel written in the Qing dynasty by Cao Xueqin (曹雪芹). Zhiyanzhai's Re-Annotations to The Story of the Stone (脂硯齋重評石頭記), known in short as Zhipi (脂批) is considered to be the most reliable version.

2 It is believed that Cao wrote the first 80 chapters. Later version of the novel in 120 chapters published jointly by later scholars Gao E (高鶚) and Cheng Weiyuan (程偉元) remains controversial.

樹洞
——詠石濤《老樹空山一坐四十小劫》

你為甚麼躲進樹洞裏？
是繪畫山水
累了
抑或，為了避風避雨
避開流行的病毒？
你難道不怕蟲蛇鼠蟻
以為挨一段日子好歹
就適應了？
你是不想走出自己的畫外？

風又來了，雨又來了
我也不想走開
能否讓我也擠進來？

Tree Hole
—— Ode to Shitao's *Sitting in a Tree Hole for 40 Kalpas*

Why are you hiding in a tree hole?
Are the tasks of painting outdoors
too arduous?
Or, you're taking refuge from the gale and the downpour
or from the ailments now ubiquitous?
Are you not afraid of all the creepy crawlies?

Are you expecting after a while
to grow accustomed?
Are you trying to stay inside your painting?

The wind is stirring, the rain is afoot
I don't want to leave either
Is it okay if I squeeze in?

我們在電腦裏的父

我們在電腦裏的父，願人都尊您的名為聖，願您在屏幕裏出現，
願我的請求、申訴，行在大街上，如同行在電腦裏。
我日常的通訊，上網，今日賜給我；
免我犯錯，如同其他匪類犯錯。
不叫我遇到黑客、死機，
拯救我脫離一切病毒。
我日常的飲食：
咖啡、三文魚、
閱讀和情愛，
全拜您所賜，
直到大停電，
開始審判。
天父及子，
及聖神
之名。
花花。

Our Father in Computer

Our Father, who art in computer, hallowed be thy name, thy image
    come on the monitor.
Grant us our requests, appeals as they will be done on the streets as on
    the screens.
Give us this day our daily internet browsing and social media.

Deliver us from trespasses committed by other sinners.

Lead us not into crashes and hackers,

and deliver us from all viruses.

My everyday sustenance:

Coffee, fillets of salmon,

reading and also loving,

all due to your grace,

until the blackout on

the Judgment Day,

In the name of

Father, Son,

Holy Spirit.

Fa-fa

我有一個噩夢

我有一個噩夢
有一天，我被長期隔離
不是因為我的膚色
而是我和隱藏的病毒
有過不足五十米距離
的接觸

我有一個噩夢
有一天，我的生活再沒有病毒
再聞不到消毒藥水的氣味
也不用戴口罩了，只有罪犯
戴上，再扯不下來
而我的手長出了蹼

我有一個噩夢
有一天，我成為了一個數字
卻在千萬人群裏被認出來
我聽到已離世的母親的提示：
你又忘了今天要吃的藥丸
這會危害你和你朋友的健康

我有一個噩夢
有一天，我看見家裏進佔了
許多不屬於我的東西
噗噗抖動，我拚命把它們扔走

扔走的原來是自己
鼻子、耳朵、嘴巴、眼睛

我的噩夢是
從一個到另一個
我一直沒有醒來

I have a nightmare

I have a nightmare
One day, I was quarantined
Not for the colour of my skin
But for the less than 50 meters'
distance with the hidden virus
I shared

I have a nightmare
One day, my life was rid of all contagions
Not a whiff of disinfecting agents
No more face masks; only for sinners
face masks, once put on, stay forever
I grew webs instead

I have a nightmare
One day, I became a number
But I was singled out from millions of others
I heard my long-deceased mother's

prompt: you are endangering yourself and friends
you forget your meds again

I have a nightmare
One day, I saw in my home
things that did not belong to me
Flipping and flapping, I hurled them away
flinging what were really mine:
nose, ears, mouth and eyes

My nightmares
go on from one to another
a long slumbering affair

別以為你的名字是玫瑰就芳香起來

玫瑰，別以為你的名字是玫瑰就芳香起來
你只是外表豔麗
好像把其他的花花草草比下去
要知道，你只吸引蜂蝶
色迷迷，誰還關心你
是否有內在美
太自覺的美
是病態
就當是名字的錯吧
你試改做新冠肺炎看看
所有人馬上嚇瘋了
避毒如仇
愛就到了盡頭
你注定名列惡棍
你外表變得醜陋
還私藏了惡毒的內心
在這裏那裏偷播病毒
你不得不東逃西竄
化裝易容；惶惶然
尋覓宿主，真的
是名字的錯麼？
照照鏡子，原來就寄生在我的另一面
如果不是較好的一半

116

Don't assume you smell great just because you're named Rose

Rose, don't assume you smell great just because you're named Rose

You are gorgeous on the outside

Better than most garden varieties, I reckon

But you know, you attract only bees and butterflies

with dubious intentions, who can't care less

if you are pretty inside

Self-conscious beauty

is a disease

The name is to blame, I suppose

Try naming yourself coronavirus

and everyone will go berserk with fear

People avoid viruses like the plague

Love will cease its existence

You are destined to be a villain

You will acquire an ungainly appearance

and harbour an evil heart within

Spreading viruses left, right and centre

you scamper and scurry

in disguise, anxiously

looking for a host. Really,

is the name to blame?

Gazing into the mirror, I find you living off my other half

Though not necessarily the better side of me

日子再久些

日子再久些，我怕
我會忘記你的樣子
限聚令下我們的距離
是愈來愈遠了
怎麼好呢，我不怕犯險只是
家長不反對，社會也不容許
我們活在你的我的口罩裏
受兩重而不同的保護
浩劫之後，我怕
再不認得彼此
我們開始懷疑
對方的性別
山變形河改道
誰還相信誓約呢，誰能確定
天堂與地獄的位置？
我怕晚上失去了月亮
早上，看不見太陽
我再不認識自己
再不認得原本生活的地方

The longer it lasts

The longer it lasts, the more
I am worried, I will forget your face

Under the social gathering ban, our distance runs
amok, away, apart from each other
What should we do? Though I'm not worried about danger
our parents frown and the city closes down
You live behind your mask and I mine
doubly and separately protected
After this calamity, I am worried
we will not recognize each other
and we will begin to doubt
each other's gender
A river changes course, a mountain its shape
Who still believes in undying vows? Who is still
certain: where's heaven and where's hell?
I am worried the moon will not be there at night
and in the morning, the sun will disappear
I am worried that I will no longer know myself
nor the place I call home all these years

疫後

瘟疫沒有過去
不客氣地留下來
但一位政客
掰開前面幾個政客
從防空洞出來
已急不及待，大喊：
這是又一次，打勝了仗
在我的領導下
馬上就會復興經濟
大家歡呼拍手
他呢，是打手
左手打右手

都出來了，一位精神領袖
曾預言世界末日
他的臉面還留下口罩的深痕，說：
這是上主走過的烙印
懺悔啊，末日又再逼近
一個女孩問：因為我多吃了糖果？

我呢，一直樂觀得緊
冬天來了，春天還不肯出來？
我一位朋友宅居時發明了
可以蒸燉的口罩
讓人帶來貼身的食材

他準備開設幾間私房菜
招牌食譜是一罩三吃

另一位在研發激光眼鏡
令病毒無所遁形，用神一瞪
可以把病毒消滅
已經進入人眼測試的階段
我趕緊提醒他申請專利權

一位富三代從隔離營取得靈感
改良了劏房
本來容納五家的空間
變成了五十家
辦法是從食物入手
把人變瘦，縮小
變成哈哈比人

一位從事教育的校友也出來了
他認定由於防毒軟件不足
病毒就來偷襲了
切要保護學童
先刪除，再貼上
保險重重
密碼，要不停更改

他當年的宿友馬上駁嘴
你從不汲取善忘的教訓
不是老在問人：改成甚麼？

這兩個活寶吵了數十年
又要找我做和事老
倘其中一個遭逢不幸
另一個的日子真不知怎樣過

還有一位，想盡辦法
和認識半年的文青女友
浪漫而和平地分手，說：
我們曾在一起誦讀聖典：
《愛在瘟疫蔓延時》
好歹愛過，如今
瘟疫快要過去
讓我們各自重新開始
別難過，真正的情人
自會在不太遙遠的
另一次瘟疫裏邂逅
這個人，就是我

Post-pandemic

The pandemic is not over
Unceremoniously, it stays
But a politician
shoving off a few fellow legislators
emerged from the shelter
of a dug-out, eagerly declared:
Once more, we won the war

Under my leadership
the economy will be restored
Everyone happily clapped hands
For him, he slapped hands
Left hand slapping the right hand

From the dug-out the rest emerged; a spiritual leader
who, Armageddon he once predicted,
with face etched deep in mask-furrows, opined:
Branded here are the marks of the Lord
Repent, the doomsday destined is nearer
A girl asked: Is it because I have too much sweets?

Me, I am forever an optimist
Winter has arrived, will Spring refuse to emerge?
A stay-at-home friend discovered
a mask that can steam and stew
with ingredients of different bodily flavours
He is going to open a few private kitchens
The signature dish is one mask in three different preparations

Another friend is researching laser lenses
that can expose viruses, and with a single glare
exterminate viruses
It has now reached human-eye testing phases
I urged him to ASAP apply for a patent

A third-generation-rich was inspired at quarantine camp

to improve upon subdivided-flats;
the space for five homes
will be transformed into a 50-home zone
with a simple hack on food
to make men smaller, shrunk
to the size of HoHoHobbits

An alma-mater friend in education also comes forward
The lack of antivirus software, he stated
enabled the virus to attack
We have to protect our students
We delete, then we attach
Protection upon protection
Password updates non-stop

His hallmate of yesteryear came back with a prompt retort
You never remember the lesson, your forgetfulness
always asking people: Change? Into what?
These two clowns have bickered for years
and me again acting as mediator
If one of them met his demise
the other might have no idea how to survive

There is also this friend, who tried everything
with his bohemian poseur girlfriend of six months
to, romantically and peacefully, break up:
We once read together the literary bible
"Love in the Time of Coronavirus"

We once loved, for better or worse

And now, the pandemic almost over

Let us begin our separate lives

Don't be sad, your genuine other half

will be waiting in the not-too-distant future

to meet you in the next pandemic

This other half will be me

問天

—— 耶和華遂後悔在地上造了人，心中很
是悲痛。(《創世紀》6：6)

上天説話
用雲，用雨水

有時我們嫌它
説得太多

上天生氣
用戰火，用地震
見人沒有改過
用病毒

往往連累了
許多的無辜

從天際俯看
看到橢圓的球體，看到
平面的城鄉與山川
看到微塵似的
人類，是否還看到
每個都不一樣？

上天不是説：
用石頭扔她吧

要是自以為從沒犯錯

人類學會了告解
學會了無差別的愛
我們，能否走過悲痛
彼此寬恕
從頭再來？

Why, Lord, why?

> ——*The LORD was sorry that He had made man on*
> *the earth, and He was grieved in His heart*
>
> *(Genesis 6:6)*

The Lord speaks
in clouds and in rainfalls

Sometimes, we are a bit miffed
He speaks in volume

Exasperated, the Lord
bellows in quakes and in wars
And, seeing no remorse,
He speaks in viruses

Implicating often
many innocents

From beyond the sky
the Lord sees our sphere, elliptical
our cities, villages, hills and rivers, two-dimensional
When He sees humans
dust-like beings, does He see
us as individual specks, all different?

Didn't the Lord announce:
He that is without sin among you
let him first cast a stone at her.

Humans have learned repentance
and universal love
Will we survive the grieve and pain
forgive each other
and start over again?

請鍾馗

請你來袪邪除鬼
但你的尊容直把我們嚇壞了
頂破帽，衣藍袍，繫角帶，蓬頭虬鬢
圓睜怒目，笏板插在腰上
活像後來小説裏的李逵
你説你本來並不那麼醜
進士出身，不過殿試落第
平生沒嘗過失敗
這是致命傷
還鄉沒有面目
就一頭撞向殿階
説時又逕啖一小鬼
其他小鬼豈敢再胡鬧
莫不乖乖下跪
之後呢，我們瞇着眼問
這就血肉下碎如泥
再拼湊不起來，當年
恰巧遇上一個小白臉的皇帝
多情善感把你厚葬
土地神打聽後上報天帝
天帝瞄了一眼你的樣子
馬上晉升你為大鬼王
管治人間眾小鬼
天廷也不需特別破費
鬧事的就當是你的口糧

我們遍查錄鬼簿
你的履歷最輝煌
你的確很醜，對不起
但心底肯定很美麗
你知道，總有些小鬼冥頑不馴
這次最狡黠的一個
隱形，無聲，化成病毒
躲在水渠，電梯，乘搭空氣
出席婚宴，參加舞會
偷襲不設防的善男信女
再幾何級分身，再分身
即使懸掛你的畫像
仍然無法驅除
求求你，人間走一趟
大駕親臨
替我們解難消災

Calling upon Zhong Kui[1], the Demon Queller

We asked you to eradicate evil and ward off devils

But your very appearance scared us the most

Horn belt, raggedy hat, blue loose robe, hair and sideburns all disheveled

Eyes burning in anger; in your waistbelt, a court board anchored

you looked like the spitting image of Li Kui[2], in fiction

You weren't that ugly to begin with, you said

You were once a Jinshi[3] scholar, but failed the imperial examination

In your whole life, you never suffered a failure

A fatal error

Now too ashamed to return home

You bashed your head against the royal staircase

Recounting the history, you took a hearty bite of a small ghost

The others at once ceased all silliness

And knelt down in earnest

What happened afterwards, we asked, squinty-eyed

The flesh and gore all minced up

Could not be patched up. A lily-livered emperor

happened to rule in those days

and a lavish teary burial for you he delivered

The village god heard and reported to the Emperor of Heaven

who, one sidelong glance at your appearance,

immediately promoted you to the rank of Top Ghost Master

in charge of all the world's spectres

As such, the Court of Heaven got to save on your keep

The unruly spirits would be your daily food ration

From a thorough check on the Ghost Chronicle[4]

You had the most impressive curriculum vitae

Ugly indeed you were, sorry to say

But you had a heart of gold

You know. There would always be incorrigible

ghosts. This one was the most duplicitous

Invisible, deathly silent, into a virus

it turned, hidden in gutters, elevators, riding on air

attending weddings and dances everywhere

to ambush unsuspecting ladies and gents

Exponential multiplication of exponential replication

Even after your portrait was hoisted

T'was not enough to dispel this virus

Please, to the human realm,

a personal visit you must make

to deliver us from our mayhem

Translator's notes:

1   Zhong Kui（鍾馗）is a mythical character in ancient Chinese folklore. Zhong is believed to be a guardian god against all ghosts and evil spirits. His portraits were hung in household as a means to ward off devils and ghosts.

2   Li Kui（李逵）is a fictional character from The Water Margin. Described as ferocious and ugly with unruly beard and sideburn.

3   Jinshi（進士）is scholar who achieved the highest and final degree in the imperial examination in Imperial China.

4   Ghost Chronicle（録鬼簿）is compiled in the Yuan Dynasty recording the life and works of Yuan "qu" opera writers.

卓古拉先生搬家

——向茂瑙（F. W. Murnau）致敬

卓古拉先生抬着他的家
那不過是幾塊殘舊的木材
到處尋找一個可以棲身的角落
那怕是偏僻、狹隘的劏房
只需避過陽光
他很焦急，害怕
天快亮了，別以為
只有別人才怕他

他原本住在羅馬尼亞山上
沒有人知道他的歲數
曾有人當他是民族英雄
後來開始了獵巫行動
他千里迢迢，跑到陌生的英國
一船瘟疫，只有他倖存
他成為了帶菌的惡魔
晝伏夜出，鬼魅似的飄泊

離開了他牢靠的古堡
為的是看了一幀少女的照片
他的原鄉不是有眾多的美少女？
有的，可沒有長而又長
多麼漂亮的頸項，那是

他的異托邦，他愛得瘋狂
太陽快出來了
他必須找到一個藏身的地方

Mister Dracula moving house
——A tribute to F.W. Murnau

Mister Dracula is carrying his home
Just a few pieces of decrepit timber
searching everywhere for a corner, for shelter
Even if it's only a remote, tiny subdivided chamber
A place to escape the sunlight
He's anxious, he's in fright
It's almost dawn. He fears
as much as he is feared

He used to live in the mountains of Romania
No one knew his age
He was once regarded a national hero
Later it began, the witch hunt
He travelled thousands of miles to faraway England
A shipful of pandemic, he alone survived
as the virus-carrying demon
Nocturnal, he wandered like a ghost

Leave his stronghold, the castle, he did
All because he saw a photo of a young girl

Isn't his hometown full of beautiful girls?

Yes, but none with a graceful neck

of such extraordinary length, for him

a heterotopia dream; he loved with all his might

The sun will soon come out

He must find a hideout

病毒移民

3000 年，風雷震作
瘟疫攻陷了地球
我們倖存者展開星際飄泊
尋覓新的家園
進入宇航船後我開始記錄：
我們化整為零，不分國族
一千家一船散佈
像億萬顆隕石，飛向
不斷膨脹的太空
就是不成功，也夠崇高、悲壯
誰先找到理想的地方
就以宇宙語通報，不過
我們馬上重新戴上面罩
保持社交警覺，因為
我們的探測器發瘋似的警示
病毒一直緊隨，潛入了
我們下一代的腦袋
再伺機擴散，所以
我們急忙在幼兒的休眠艙
進行搶救，重新改造
抗疫多年，全盤失敗
我們終於領悟，最好的對策
不是解毒，而是以毒攻毒
輸無可輸，輸入適量的病毒
令新生代比病毒狡點得更病毒

令病毒，後悔跟隨我們移民

3070 年，我們仍然在星際流浪
尋覓那怕是不那麼理想的地方
其他的宇航船已經失聯
空寂，無垠的宇宙
曾有過幾艘落腳的消息
最後是失望，徹底地
船毀人亡，而我們
成為了最後的餘生
苦悶，疲累，垂垂老去
我們的氧氣急劇減少
只餘下一個月，因為
要和愈來愈多的新生病毒分享
不能多，也決不能少
彼此勉強維持
食物也逐漸短缺
開始嚴格分配
我們吃的，是打印的藥丸
然後和排洩循環再造
簡單恐怖，但有甚麼辦法呢
我們都瘦弱得不似人形了
失去說話的力氣
話語，其實也成為禁忌
病毒充滿猜疑，敵意
全賴疏通一點血緣
也不會笨得殺光宿主

當我們和病毒頭頭靖綏
那晚上，我筋疲力盡
難得沉沉睡去
我做了一個好夢
到了那麼一個地方
城市非常整潔好看
有一座凱旋門
一座羅浮宮，一兩座
金字塔馬丘比丘
長城在山上不斷延長
病毒組長說，想有甚麼可以商量
有問題也可以向組長通報
家中的洗手間有一條長江
一條好脾氣的黃河
食物立體還原，自然消毒
水很潔淨，分三種
很好、極好、最好
誰不指望活得最好前提是
活着；我們到醫療室脫下面罩
空氣太清新了，肺許久才適應
我們學會對一切寬容
學會如何整齊地散步
讚賞病毒的領導
我回到了和女友分手的時候
她去了非洲當無國籍醫生
五年後，幸得不死
我們從頭再來
然後是六七歲

我在公園裏踢球，大口吃掉
妹妹手上的冰淇淋
仰頭看，那是久違了的月亮
它多麼寧靜、祥和
我背誦母親教我的「但願人長久」
她慈愛地向我微笑
我本來已忘了她的樣子了
我不再做記錄，才五個月大胎兒
輕踢了母親的肚子，卻看到
父親一臉的愁思

Virus emigrants

Year 3000, in squalls and thunders

the pandemic besieged the Earth

We survivors embarked on an interstellar wander

in search for a new home

In the spacecraft, I started recording:

We broke into groups, regardless of roots

A thousand families per ship we scattered

like hundreds of millions of meteors, flying towards

the ever-expanding universe

It might not be successful, but a noble and tragic mission it was

Whoever first found the ideal location

would send a cosmic-language communication, but

we had to re-mask immediately

Keep social watchfulness, because

our detectors went crazy with alerts

The virus had been following us, sneaking in

to the heads of our young generation

waiting for an opportunity to proliferate, so

we rushed into the toddler sleeping cabins

to conduct rescues, and to organize reforms

For many years we had fought the virus, to no avail

We finally realized; the best strategy was

not to neutralize, but to fight virus with virus

We had nothing to lose; let loose the right amount of virus

to make our new generation more viral than the last virus

Make the virus regret ever emigrating with us

In 3070, we were still wandering the galaxy

In search for a place, even if it was not the most ideal

The other spacecrafts had lost contact

in the immense, empty universe

We heard of touch-downs from several ships in fact

But they proved to be disappointing news; utterly

these ships and crews were wrecked, and we

became the last lives remaining

Dejected, exhausted, slowly withering

Our oxygen was radically reduced

Only enough for a month was left, because

it had to be shared with more and more new viruses

Not too much, not too little either

Just enough to maintain each other

Food supply became scant

Strict rationing began

What we ate were 3D-printed tablets

and later upcycled from recycled excrement

Crude and abhorrent, but there were no other methods

We were so thin and frail, we no longer resembled human

And we lost the power of speech

Speaking, besides, had become taboo

The virus was full of suspicion and hostility

Thank goodness there was still the symbiotic link

It wouldn't be stupid enough to kill off the hosts

When we and the virus leaders reached a peace agreement

That night, I was exhausted

Fell into a deep slumber

I dreamed a good dream

We arrive at a place

a neat and tidy city

We have an Arc de Triomphe

a Louvre museum, a pyramid

or two and a Machu Picchu

The Great Wall meanders endlessly on the mountains

The virus leader says everything can be deliberated

Any problem we encounter, we can report to the virus leader

At our home the bathroom is equipped with a Yangtze River

and an obliging Yellow River with excellent temper

The food, 3-dimensional, sterilizes itself

Water is very clean and comes in 3 tiers

Good, Very-Good, The-Goodest

Who wouldn't want a Goodest life, but we need to first stay

alive; we go to the medical room to take off the mask

The air is so fresh, it takes the lungs a while to acclimatize

We learn to tolerate, to take it easy

Learn how to take a stroll neatly

and appreciate the leadership of the virus

I go back in time to when I broke up with my girlfriend

She went to Africa as a doctor without borders

Five years later, fortunately she's still alive

And we start over

Then I go back to when I was six or seven years old

I play football in the park and steal a bite of ice cream

from the hand of my sister

Looking up, the long-lost moon emerges

So peaceful, so serene

I recite the line my mother taught me "May we endure..."

She smiles lovingly at me

I have forgotten her looks

I no longer keep records, now a fetus of barely five months

I give my mother's tummy a shove, and see

on my father, a look of sadness

航向伊薩卡

當你起航前往伊薩卡
但願你的旅途漫長，
充滿冒險，充滿發現。
萊斯特律戈涅斯巨人，獨眼巨人，
憤怒的波塞冬海神——不要怕他們：
你將不會在路上碰到諸如此類的怪物。
　　　　——卡瓦菲斯：〈伊薩卡島〉（1911）

隨着詩人的旅程，容我打岔
就是遇到巨人、海神
（我不知道原來他的脾氣不好）
有甚麼好怕呢，你進入了
神話的國度
以往你只在書本上讀到
在夢中曾到，橄欖樹、古陶瓶
伊卡洛斯忘形地飛近太陽
丟落一片蔚藍的愛琴海
如今，你隨着詩句
航向尤里西斯的故鄉
他是飄泊後歸途，疲累，衰頹
你呢，打開靈視的眼界
從埃及到希臘，上窮碧落
為蒼生尋找解藥
一種邪氣正在天地間肆虐
豈不是《伊底帕斯王》的序幕？

你靜聽，還可以聽到妖媚的歌聲
那些歌聲，連天帝也會為之失神
叫你留下來，終止尋覓
這，才是你真正的考驗
別忘了你為甚麼上路
沒有一個地方是樂土
沒有一個地方沒有危險、困阻
只要你堅持，勇敢
巨人、海神不會把你打倒
你甚至會降服那頭半人半牛
的怪物，走出迷宮
藉着一條柔韌堅致的線索
從東方到西方
帶引你找到解藥

Set sail for Ithaka

As you set out for Ithaka
hope your road is a long one,
full of adventure, full of discovery.
Laistrygonians, Cyclops,
angry Poseidon—don't be afraid of them:
you'll never find things like that on your way
　　—*Ithaka* (1911) by C. P. CAVAFY
　　Translated by Edmund Keeley

On this journey with the poet, allow me to interject

What if you encounter Poseidon, Cyclops

(I didn't know of his temper tantrums)

What are you afraid of? You have entered

mythical kingdoms

Seeing things you've only ever read in books

Going places you've only dreamed of; olive trees, ancient potteries

entranced Icarus flying too close to the sun

falling into a blue sweep of the Aegean Sea

Now, on the trail of the verses

you set sail for the land of Ulysses

He returns home after a weary journey, worn-out and waning

And you, through your all-seeing vision

from Egypt to Greece, from the sky to the sea

you set out to find the antidote for the sorrowful masses

An evil spirit is raging from heaven to earth

It is the prologue of *Oedipus*, isn't it?

Listen, you can still hear the alluring songs

This singing, transfixes even the God of Heaven

urges you to stay and stop searching

This, is the ultimate trial

Don't forget why you are on the road

There is no paradise on earth

There is no place without danger or dearth

With forbearance and fortitude

You will withstand Giants and Poseidon

You may even conquer the half ox half man

Minotaur and exit the maze

By a ball of pliable and pertinacious cues

from East to West

you will find the path to the cure

水鳥和蘆葦的對話

我聽到一隻水鳥和蘆葦的對話：

多謝你伸直腰，向我招手；不然我會去錯地方。

　　就怕你不再到來；這裏的沼澤，的確跟其他的再沒有分別。

是病毒不好，魚蝦少了，彈塗魚和招潮蟹都躲起來。

　　或者到了另一個紅雨林，也不容易啊。

是的，但這是我來去熟悉的地方。

　　只怕很快就會變得陌生。

那麼你的日子怎麼過？

　　怎麼過？我可以成簾成蓆，葦穗化作掃帚，我還用空莖唱歌。

疫情嚴峻，你可仍然充滿正能量。

　　是的，我的問題不過是，我會思想。而且，

而且甚麼？

　　我土生土長。

Dialogue between the Waterbird and the Reed

I overheard a dialogue between the Waterbird and the Reed:

Thank you for straightening up and beckoning; else I would have gone
to the wrong patch.

　　Glad you made it; this marshland now indeed looks no different
　　from the rest.

All down to the virus, fewer fish, fewer shrimps, mudskippers and fiddler crabs are all in distress.

Maybe they have moved to another mangrove forest. Life is hard here.

Maybe, but this area I frequent is what I know best.

Soon you won't recognize it from the rest.

So, what are your plans?

What plans? I can turn myself into curtains and mats, my ears into brooms and I sing with the hollow stems.

The pandemic is prohibitive, but you are still so positive.

Yes, but my problem is, I can reason, and…

And what?

And this is my patch.

後記

寫在瘟疫蔓延時

　　大家不妨當這些詩是一篇長而又長的散文，又或者是綴段式短而又短的小說，只不過都分了行。這些分行的東西，講的是 2020 一年瘟疫蔓延的故事。所以也不妨當是紀錄。這場瘟疫是世界性的，無分貧富，許多城一度因疫情嚴峻而封了，城裏的人不容出外，城外的人不許進來。說來分明是小說的情境：圍城之下，外人想進來，內人想出去。前人寫過，就是還不曾用詩分行的形式寫一書本。我不是悲觀的人，——相反，朋友說悲劇到了我手上，會變成喜劇，有時甚至變成鬧劇。我無法辯解，只能引用《西遊記》的孫行者遇到困難時所言：哭不得，只好笑。我不以為瘟疫會真的過去，不會的，它不過玩乏了，躲起來，韜光一陣，變換一個樣子，以增強版再來。世間事往往是這樣，你以為夠壞的了，誰知還有更壞要來。

　　詩末沒有註明寫作日期，我可是隨着疫情的發展而寫，也照這樣編排次序，例如防疫的口罩，遲至三四月也許因為不敷應用吧，世衛仍然說「無病不需戴」，於是戴了的人，就被視為感染者，變得生人勿近，這是其中一首〈加拿大來郵〉的由來。又如〈瘋劫〉，寫匪徒搶劫超市幾百卷廁紙，外地的朋友或嫌荒謬，太誇張，卻是二月間本地發生的實況。瘟疫期間，謠言滿天，人們甚麼都搶購，也就甚麼都搶劫。當然，我也希望不止於時事的紀錄，因為事過境遷，太貼地，到頭來就變成離地。我希望做到既寫實，又寫意；記瘟疫，又不止於瘟疫。而故事，何曾煞科。以香港來說，一波未平，一波又起，到年底十二月爆發更凶險的第四波。

我們和病毒結緣，結的一直是不解緣，真是山無陵，江水竭；冬雷震震，夏雨雪，天地合，乃敢與君絕。事實上，病毒、細菌，是我們的長輩，比人類的歷史悠久得多；說是病毒，那是人類的看法。人類在不同的時間空間替它起過不同的名字：黑死病、天花、瘧疾、梅毒、黃疸、肺結核……，目前肆虐全球的則叫新冠肺炎。連名字也各有爭議；病毒，首先入侵政治。它比人聰明，狡點，肯學習，會演進，在人類懂得智能之前，它已是生化智能，在大自然裏原本和人類共存，只是當平衡受到破壞，才變成結怨。而破壞這種諧協，往往是人類自己。

病毒不會輸，幸好它也從沒有贏過，沒有把人類殺光，人類也未至窩囊得舉手投降。但它改寫過人類的歷史，也正在改變當下人類的發展，大如國際的政局、利益的分配，不是在變，在大變麼？人類呢，我忝為其中之一，如果沒有退步，也不過在繞圈，不斷重蹈覆轍。看人類獵殺捕食的醜態就足以知道。十七年前，2003 年，因為吃野生動物，產生非典，香港一千七百多人染病，近三百人死亡；全球計，則感染者八千多人，死亡八百多人。2020 一年，從年初到年底，全球確診感染新冠肺炎，人數已達八千萬，死亡人數為一百多萬，而方興未艾。

香港有過沙士的前科，但政府官僚的決策很糟糕，很難說服人這是「沒有最好，只有更好」，要是跟其他非華裔地區比較，感染與死亡的人數不高，那是醫護人員的努力，加上一般市民的自覺，香港可能是最早也最多人配戴口罩的地方。歐美以及拉美等重災區，新聞片所見，人來人去，沒戴口罩的人不少。一味鼓吹個人自由，自尊而不自律，當面對一個無形無聲的敵人，必須齊心協力，否則就要付出代價。這說明沒有一種政制是完美的。

何況，人的記憶很薄弱，或因抗疫疲勞，有些更是刻意刪除，結果瘟疫並未遏止，更有變種之虞。年初屏幕上曾傳出一個年輕女子示範吃蝙蝠的影片，我嚇了一大跳，如果窮餓得要命還差可解釋；這樣看，我們未必勝過遠古的猿人。今人為甚麼不汲取教訓呢？我想，這是因為沒有把教訓好好地記下來。我們要報喜，其實更要牢牢記憂。

在瘟疫蔓延期間，我乖乖的甚少外出，重讀一些典籍，也嘗試用詩的形式寫下這些東西。詩是從俗的叫法。我從不以為詩是各種文學創作裏的冠冕，——冠冕之說，那是封建時代的叫法，於今仍然奉行，從未立憲，例如當代的布羅茨基（Joseph Brodsky），他認為詩高於散文，詩人高於作家。他有一個有趣的說法：詩人窮了會寫文章，但散文家窮了，不會寫詩。因為詩的稿酬少得多，又往往被拖欠。順着稿酬的角度講，詩人窮了應該寫小說，更要寫史特恩《項狄傳》那種布愈拉愈長的小說，假定仍有人願意出版這種小說。至於小說家窮了，他當然不會寫詩，他為甚麼會寫詩呢？除非真的餓瘋了。他不如到快餐店當外賣，不用費神用壞了腦袋。

我當然明白布羅茨基的意思：詩人駕馭文字的能力最高，無所不擅。這是踵武雪萊的英國遺風，頌揚詩人有特權，可以為萬物萬事命名；又近承俄國的傳統，認定詩在文學創作的階層上最高。詩的國度，豈容其他作家入境污染。此外，這是以為散文、小說容易寫。誠然，詩的每一句，豈不都是散文。但以為散文隨便可以寫得好，對不起，有這種想法，則詩也不會好。二十世紀以來，小說的成果也許比詩豐碩，表現了更豐富的內容，讀者呢，更多許多。我日常乘搭交通工具，難得遇見年輕人低頭不看手機而是看書，倘是文學，看的總是小說，從魔幻到科幻，可從未見人看的是詩集。文學雜誌的銷量少，詩刊是更少。詩人難道認定這完全是社會的錯？何況，有些詩人一寫散文，就露了底，原來一直躲在晦澀、似通實不通的句子裏。

布羅茨基的詩非常好，不然怎麼可以取得諾貝爾文學獎；他的散文也毫不遜色，不然怎麼可以多次入選「全美年度最佳散文」（The Best American Essays）。不過，我們可不要盡信甚麼詩選、散文選，還要看負責選的人，選的態度。我想，無論寫散文或小說，要是不肯放下詩人的自吹自擂，加上藝術良知的重責，都很難致富。這根本就不是致富的行當。布羅茨基曾被蘇聯政府指控無所事事而坐牢，因為詩人你說你有poetic licence，可哪來的證明書？到後來他不得不移居美國。

我不認為詩高於其他文類，詩自然也不低於其他文類，而是各擅勝場，要針對不同的戰場。在這個瘟疫的時勢局面，要是以詩的形式寫作，而企圖表現當下的各方面，就要摒棄過去吾國人那種春風秋月的詩意，或者法國人那種「純詩」的觀念，而要借助散文、小說、戲劇，以至一切有效的形式。詩的國度，不容其他作家入境，詩人卻可以也必須出境周遊，打開視野。簡言之，必須打破那種文類的界限。面對疫情，要不斷洗手，但文類的潔癖則不可有，一無束縛，要怎樣寫就怎樣寫。

本書恰好共收五十首，大家就當這五十首的東西是甚麼都好，要怎麼讀就怎麼讀，它們只不過有一個共通的主題：瘟疫。

感謝沈鄧可婷女士（Teresa Shen）的翻譯，她是我許多年前的舊同事，中英文俱佳，我說笑：這本書至少有一半還是不錯的。也感謝余穎欣小姐，她在疫症期間透過電腦屏幕，以鉛筆的筆觸繪畫出一種時間感，微妙地呈現光影的效果，儼如當下狀態的記錄。她還替我設計封面。這本書是三個人抗疫時分頭合作的成果。

2020 年 12 月

2021 年 2 月 8 日補記：這書付印時，全球感染新冠肺炎的人數已過億，死亡人數超過 230 萬；美國是最重災區，病歿 46 萬，超越二戰時美軍的陣亡人數。

Postscript: In the midst of COVID-19 Pandemic

You may wish to treat this anthology of poems as an exceptionally long essay, or an exceedingly abbreviated novella. The only difference is that the poems are divided into lines. These lines tell the stories of the pandemic in 2020. In a way, they are records of the time. The pandemic affects everyone in the world, rich or poor. Many cities experienced lock-down due to the severity of the pandemic; people in the city were forbidden to leave, and people outside the city were not allowed to enter. The situation is undoubtedly the plot for a novel. In a *fortress besieged* [1], people within wanted out, and people outside wanted in. It is a storyline that has been explored, only that it has not been written in the form of a "novel-in-verses". I am not a pessimist - on the contrary, my friends often say that, in my hands, a tragedy will become a comedy, sometimes even a farce. I can't explain myself; I can only quote what Monkey King in *Journey to the West* [2] said when he encountered difficulties: I can't cry, I might as well laugh. I don't think the pandemic will really disappear; it won't. It may get bored, or it may subside or it may need to recharge itself, but it will come back in another, perhaps stronger, version. Often in life, things have a tendency to go from bad to worse. You think it's bad? The worse is yet to come.

I did not indicate the date of writing of individual poems, but they were written along with the development of the pandemic and they are presented in this order in the anthology. For example, there was limited supply of face masks in March and April of 2020. The World Health Organization insisted then that "masks aren't necessary unless one is sick", so people who wore them were regarded as infectious and were shunned. This is the background of one of the poems, "Letter from Canada", depicting the prevailing situation at the time it was written. Another example is "Batty Heist", a poem about the robbery of hundreds of toilet paper rolls in the supermarket. People from outside of Hong Kong may find it ridiculous and greatly exaggerated, but it was a local event in February. During the pandemic, rumours abound, people rush to stockpile, and even to rob. Naturally, I hope the poetry is not confined to simply being a record of current events. Circumstances change, and what was once a faithful record will become irrelevant over time. What I hope to achieve is a balance between what happened in reality and what happened in our consciousness; in other words, to record the pandemic and beyond. And these stories, they are not done being told. In Hong Kong, one wave followed at the heel of the last. In December this year, we saw the arrival of the fourth and more dangerous wave.

We have always lived inextricably alongside viruses and bacteria in a close-knit relationship. The kind of relationship that, *"until mountains lose their peaks, rivers void of water; until thunder rumbles in winter, snow falls in summer; until the heaven and earth united as one, do we part*"[3] type of relationship. Viruses and bacteria are actually our seniors. They have a much longer history than human beings. We humans may give them labels, but that is entirely our views alone. At different time and place, we have called diseases by different names: Black Death, smallpox, malaria, syphilis, jaundice, tuberculosis… and now this pandemic that caused havoc globally is called COVID-19. Even names of diseases are controversial. The virus infected first and foremost human politics. Viruses are certainly smarter, more cunning, more willing to learn and to evolve. Before humans developed intelligence, viruses had already flourished into biologically and chemically advanced beings. They have always maintained a state of coexistence with humans. When this delicate balance is upset, we stand on opposing ends. The truth of the matter is, it is often human beings ourselves who destroy the harmony.

Viruses won't lose. Fortunately, they have never won either, or they would have killed us all; nor have humans just rolled over and surrendered. Nevertheless, viruses have had the capacity to rewrite human history, and they are also changing the present development of mankind. Wouldn't you agree that, under the pandemic, current international politics and national priorities are not only changing, but undergoing significant transformation? As for human beings, myself included, if we aren't in regression, we are at best going around in circles, repeating the same mistakes over and over again. One only has to look at the ugliness of human being's predatory and gluttonous behaviour. In 2003, 17 years ago, as a result of wild animal consumption, SARS infected more than 1,700 people and killed 300 in

Hong Kong; globally, more than 8,000 people were infected and over 800 people died. In 2020, within barely twelve months, more than 80 million people worldwide were diagnosed with the new coronavirus pneumonia, COVID-19, resulting in over a million deaths. And the new pandemic is still going strong.

With the history of SARS in the background, the Hong Kong administration nonetheless came up with questionable decision-making and responses. It is difficult to convince Hong Kong residents that the actions taken thus far are "not the best but getting better". Compared with other non-Chinese areas, the infection and fatality rates in Hong Kong have remained relatively low. This was largely due to the diligence of the medical communities and the conscientiousness of the Hong Kong people. Hong Kong is probably the earliest city where most residents wear masks. In the hardest-hit areas in Europe, America and Latin America, as seen in news footages, people go about their daily life without mask. Advocating personal freedom and dignity at the expense of discipline, in the face of an invisible and silent enemy that requires concerted efforts, is bound to take a heavy toll. Evidently, no political system is perfect.

What's more, people have short memories, and due to pandemic fatigue, some have chosen not to remember, giving the viruses a chance to return; and return they do in a more infectious variant. At the beginning of 2020, a video of a young woman demonstrating how to eat bats went viral. I was totally shocked. Abject poverty or extreme hunger may justify such behaviour, but as it is, we are hardly better than our ancient forebears, the primates. Why won't we learn? To me, the reason is these lessons have not been taken in properly and in their entirety. We need to stop deceiving ourselves and really commit to memory the bad as well as the good.

During the pandemic, I dutifully stayed home to re-read classics and to record my thinking in verses. Poetry is a lay person's designation. I never thought that poetry was the crown of literary creations - this hierarchical theory that poetry is superior to prose is an antiquated thinking that, though never sanctioned, is still going strong today. Joseph Brodsky, a contemporary, considered poetry above prose and poets superior to writers. He had an interesting saying: "the cash-strapped poet can sit down and write an article; while the novelist in the same situation can hardly conceive of a poem … poetry is paid much less and more slowly, than prose." Speaking from the perspective of remuneration, poets should write novels when they are strapped for cash, and they should write long, filibustering novels of the length of the like of Laurence Sterne's *The Life and Opinions of Tristram Shandy, Gentleman*. That is assuming that people are still willing to publish such novels. As for the poor novelist, he certainly will not write poetry. Why should he? Unless his hunger has robbed him of his senses. He will be better off delivering takeaway for fast food shops; and save his brains from being overused.

I do understand what Brodsky meant: the poet has the best command of language and he excels in all its forms. This echoes the British legacy of Shelley. Shelley idealized the divine power of the poet who alone is able to interpret cosmic truth; and closely follows the Russian traditional belief that poetry is the highest form in the literary hierarchy. In short, the kingdom of poetry is off-limit to other writers who may otherwise pollute its sanctity. In addition, there is the perception that prose and novel are easy to write. Of course, when you break it down, every line of a poem is but a part of a prose. But to assume that good prose is easy to come by, I'm sorry, is the kind of misconception that prevents one from achieving good poetry. Since the twentieth century, novel as a genre has undoubtedly achieved much more than poetry, showing a richer content, embracing more innovative forms of narratives and, needless to say, having many more readers. Poetry, on the other hand, has remained largely unchanged. I usually take public transports, and I rarely see young people reading books instead of looking at their phones. If they are indeed reading books, these will invariably be novels, usually fantasy or science fiction. I have never seen people reading poetry. Literary magazines are low in circulation, and poetry periodicals fare far worse. Do poets seriously believe that all this is society's fault? What's more, some poets, should they venture into the realms of prose, could well be exposed as having been hiding under obscure and dubious literary constructions all along.

Brodsky's poems are undeniably excellent, otherwise he would not be a Nobel Prize winner in Literature; his prose is no less brilliant either, otherwise his works would not have been repeatedly selected as The Best American Essays. Naturally we will not take whatever poetry selections or random best novel lists at their face value; a lot depends on the composition of the panels and their mandates. However, regardless of the genre, prose or novel, if one refuses to let go of the poet's pride, coupled with the burden of artistic conscience, it is difficult to achieve success. The literary path is never one to achieve riches to begin with. In fact, Brodsky was once jailed by the Soviet government for social parasitism. Poetic license was not something easily certifiable. Later Brodsky had no choice but to move to the United States.

I don't think poems are better than other genres, and naturally, nor is poetry inferior to other genres. It is a matter of "to each his own", both in terms of strengths and challenges. In this time of pandemic, if one is to write in the form of poetry to capture all aspect of the "present", one has to abandon the "spring moon and autumn breeze" type of lyricism so popular with our fellow countrymen, or the concept of "la poésie pure" embraced by the French Symbolists. One has to resort to prose, novel, drama, and whatever other forms that are effective. The kingdom of poetry may not allow other writers to enter, but the poet can travel freely outside to broaden his horizon and learn from other literary forms. In short, the boundaries of genre must be broken. In the face of the epidemic, we must wash our hands constantly, but the obsession of cleansed genres should not exist. Write whatever you want without boundary.

There are 50 poems in this anthology. Read these pieces as whatever you fancy, read them the way your heart desires. They only have one theme in common: the plague – written in the time of a global pandemic.

A word of thanks to Teresa Shen for translating the collection. She is an old colleague who has good command of both the English and Chinese languages. I jokingly told her that at least half of the book was not bad. I am also thankful to Yu Wingyan. She stayed home during the pandemic and created, through the computer, graphite strokes that captured a sense of time, a delicate juxtaposition of light and dark and a record of the current circumstances. She is also the designer of the book cover. This anthology is the collective work of three people's individual fight against the pandemic.

December, 2020

161

February 8, 2021 supplementary notes: When this book went to press, the number of coronavirus infection worldwide had exceeded 100 million, and the death toll went over 2.3 million; the United States was the hardest-hit country, with 460,000 deaths, surpassing the number of US fallen soldiers during World War II.

Translator's notes:
1   Fortress Besieged (圍城) is a 1947 satirical novel written by Qian Zhongshu (錢鍾書).
2   Journey to the West (西遊記) is a classical novel written in the Ming dynasty at around 16th century and attributed to Wu Cheng'en (吳承恩).
3   Extract from Shangye (上邪), a Han dynasty poem in the Collection of Yuefu Lyric Poems (樂府詩集) compiled by Guo Maoqian (郭茂倩) of the Sung Dynasty.

訪何福仁談《孔林裏的駐校青蛙》

李浩榮

問：李浩榮
何：何福仁
（日期：2020 年 2 月 9 日）

何福仁新近出版詩集《孔林裏的駐校青蛙》，收錄新詩
七十首，題材廣泛，大如宇宙行星、美墨圍牆、地產霸
權，小似寵物花貓、窗邊麻雀，皆能入題。形式方面，
極具創新，既以詩發議論，又以小說入詩，從嶄新的角
度，重閱新聞，重註經典。

一、形式

問：《孔林裏的駐校青蛙》很多作品均以詩發議論，而且涉及
政治、地產、宇宙等大課題，以詩發議論，有何優勢？

何：沒有甚麼優勢，當然也沒有甚麼劣勢，就看你想表達甚
麼。我不過是詩裏有些想法罷了。但「理」是不能乾巴巴
地「說」的，要借重美學的修辭，所以我往往嘗試設喻一
個情景，扮演一個角色，……。集中我也寫過好像是抒
情的東西吧。

一位朋友曾跟我談起刊在《羅盤》上的〈詩中議論〉，問
我在文集裏何以不收，因為我的《羅盤》不知放在哪裏去
了，以為是一篇短文，朋友影印給我，原來也不短，開
宗明義說：

詩中議論，可分廣義和狹義兩種，前者是詩人對
人生世相的觀察，是自然普遍的常規，稱之為「哲
理」；後者是特定時空下道德或事物的準則，因應環
境，我稱之為「義理」。

話很平常，有人曾在一本甚麼詩選裏徵引，我自己也看
得不明不白，原來訛誤不加校對。此文寫於四十年前，
引用不少古今中外的詩例，說明歷來詩作大不乏議論。
「對人生世相的觀察」云云，還可以加上「體悟」。我如
今覺得，抒情與議論不是對立的，更不應強分。從廣
義的角度看，你很難找到一首純粹抒情而不帶議論成分
的詩，找到了，就必定是好詩嗎？記得楊牧有一文論唐
詩的敍事性，指出唐以前的詩，儘管來源不同，形式有
異，總是明顯地趨向敍事；《詩經》的三種經典手法，敍
述鋪陳的「賦」，比較「興」和「比」更有決定性的意義。

164

問：宋詩也以重知性、擅議論見稱，您的散文寫過黃庭堅，對於宋詩，有沒有甚麼心得？

何：哪有心得，只是雜亂無章地讀書，不過我有一點懷疑精神。黃庭堅說：「小詩，文章之末，何足甚工。」這是言不由衷，江西詩派講究文字推敲，要字字有來歷。他的詩，包括他的字，都講究法度。錢鍾書的《宋詩選註》，說宋詩喜歡講道理，愛發議論，是缺陷之一。他選得很有個性，最精彩的是他的前言、對詩家的分析，許多妙趣的比喻，我當散文看，但作為選集，坦白說，並不周全。他沒選僧人、理學家的詩，隨便舉一個例吧，僧志南的《絕句》：

古木陰中繫短篷，杖藜扶我過橋東。
沾衣欲濕杏花雨，吹面不寒楊柳風。

下聯就非常好，杏花雨沾衣而未濕、楊柳風吹面而不寒。比選集中大部分的詩都要好。後來明代科舉第一的羅洪先也這樣寫：「東風吹雨衣不濕，我在桃花深處行。」差多了。禪趣，正是前人少見，宋人較多。當然，宋詩的好作品，大多走到詞那裏去了。我想，這和議論無關。唐人，以至詩騷、樂府，不議論麼？可以說，我們沒有一個不議論的詩人，或者一本不議論的詩集。轉變的，其實是範式。同樣的五言七言，唐人寫了幾乎三百年，兩杜三李，還有韓白、邊塞詩人，豈能超越。我那篇文字，引了葉燮《原詩》外篇，指出伸唐而絀宋不對。倘不嫌叨嚕，不妨加引：

從來論詩者，大約伸唐而絀宋。有謂「唐人以詩為詩，主性情，於三百篇為近；宋人以文為詩，主議論，於三百篇為遠。」何言之謬也！唐人詩有議論者，杜甫是也。杜五言古，議論尤多。長篇如〈赴奉先縣詠懷〉、〈北征〉及〈八哀〉等作，何首無議論？而獨以議論歸宋人，何歟？彼先不知何者是議論，何者為非議論，而妄分時代邪？且三百篇中，二雅為議論者，正自不少。彼先不知三百篇，安能知後人之詩也！如言宋人以文為詩，則李白樂府長短句，何嘗非文。杜甫〈前、後出塞〉及〈潼關吏〉等篇，其中豈無似文之句？為此言者，不但未見宋詩，並未見唐詩。

嚴羽《滄浪詩話》貶斥江西詩派的「以文字為詩，以才學為詩，以議論為詩」，要人學《楚辭》，而不論《詩經》。《楚辭》文字、才學、議論三者都有，當然還有恢宏的想像力，美人芳草，沒有的反而是他鼓吹「羚羊掛角，無跡可求」的禪趣。這是一家之言，以為是唯一準則，就成為一家之偏。古代詩論中講文學發展的源流正變，還是《原詩》比較全面而有系統。

由此看來，從四言、五言，到七言，唐詩宋詞元曲，一直在發展、改變形式，你可以說這是審美內容的推動，其實也是詩體的掙扎求存。到了五四，新詩徹底打破形式的束縛，是正確而必須。

科學上的種種突破，是打破舊思維、舊做法。這是範式轉移，文學藝術何嘗不是，不過科學要決絕得多。

問：詩集裏，有以小說形式寫成的詩，如〈科幻年代〉寫一場滑稽的劫機事件，〈寓言〉寫一個唯恐天下不亂的國王，〈2066 年〉以科幻的方式書寫未來，以此形式寫詩，怎樣呈現詩的特色？

何：最近伊朗軍方擊落烏航客機，承認是人為失誤所致。這樣看〈科幻年代〉就並不滑稽，並不虛幻。過去不是有過若干客機不明不白墜毀，或者失蹤？近年我看了些有關科幻的書，好的科幻作品，寫不是不止是將來，根本就是現在。這是前人詩作裏還來不及處理的題材，我們生活在科技操控的時代，我自然而然寫了這些，並沒有刻意為之。詩集中其實許多首都有這種「科幻」色彩。

詩的形式是沒有限制的，可以伸向小說、戲劇，扮演角色……。

問：辛波絲卡也擅長以故事入詩，而您與素葉同人，早於七八十年代，便引入東歐詩歌來港，東歐的詩歌對您寫作有沒有影響？

何：年輕時喜歡不少東歐詩人，例如Holan、Seifert，波蘭除了辛波絲卡，至少還有米沃什（Miłosz）和赫伯特（Zbigniew Herbert）。這果然是「國家不幸詩家幸，賦到滄桑句便工」。他們許多都有話要說。他們對我的影響，應該是有的，但我說不清楚。鄭樹森、黃繼持八十年代編《八方》時，也辦過東歐文學特輯，比較深入。我是否也受命譯過一兩首詩？

寫詩，是有話要說。不過，如果認為只有表現國家不幸的才是詩人，才是作家，也是另一種專制。辛波絲卡關心的，就別有天地了。戰爭是短暫的，巧克力是永恆的。

問：詰問、諷刺、反語，是您新詩裏常見的修辭，由此流露出一種遊戲人間的心態，運用這些手法，有甚麼好處？

何：這可能由於個人的脾性，也和社會的變化有關，要說是好處，還得看是否切合內容，手法並沒有保證。

二、中國經典

問：《孔林裏的駐校青蛙》中，不少詩作均在重新詮釋經典，如〈愚公移山〉，傳統的解讀，一般把愚公當作勤勞的模範，但您詩裏的愚公，卻成了悲劇人物，遺禍子孫，為甚麼會有這樣的看法？

何：愚公移山的道理，是教訓我們要不怕困難，堅持不懈地苦幹，就會成功。沒有人會反對這道理，問題在好道理要找到好例證，倘不適切就會有反效果。移山的故事，千瘡百孔，詩中種種質疑，是小朋友也會提出的。他最後沒有一愚到底，擺脫了悲劇的宿命。我們用散文，用小說，用評論去反省舊經典、舊道德，為甚麼不可以用詩？

問：〈祝英臺〉〈梁山伯〉更以性別理論的新視野重讀「梁祝」，一題兩寫，您認為梁祝的悲劇性在哪裏？

何：祝英臺真有其人，各種傳聞都集中在渲染他們的愛情悲劇，到頭來強化了舊禮教、舊道德。而忽略了祝英臺是一個追求自由意志的人物，千年前在男尊女卑的社會，十來歲時女扮男裝，離家苦心求學。這是對知識的醒覺，對身份的質疑，是歷史上最大的突破，比木蘭從軍更有意思。

在當代某些文學藝術，也可見一些心理學的挪用，實質是父權作祟，連女性學者也內化了這種視角，至於草根式掛羊頭賣狗肉的電影更不用說了。

問：〈孔林裏的駐校青蛙〉寫孔子學說在闡釋上的分歧，眾聲喧嘩，這方面您有沒有甚麼的研究？

何：幾年前重訪曲阜，寫過一篇〈孔子訪孔林〉，孔子和《論語》，我一直很有興趣，《論語》反覆讀了數十年，因為讀不懂，這才有趣。我另外還寫過兩篇，文章較長，都過萬字，還沒有發表，因為其他工作，擱起來了。我想多寫幾篇，湊成一本書，題目可以是其中一篇，叫《我所不知道的〈論語〉》。

三、西方經典

問：天使、上帝、天堂、創世等課題，在多首詩作中均有處理，如〈寂寞的天使〉質疑天使的僭越，〈孩子的禱告〉反思天堂的性質及上帝的角色，〈弗蘭肯斯坦〉重新詮釋《創世紀》，能談談您對這四項基督教觀念的思索嗎？

何：宗教觀念之外，這些詩，還想到其他。我想，一個不容宗教信仰自由的國度會很可憐，但宗教信仰太激烈，卻很可怕。我在宗教家庭長大，在宗教學校讀書，我父親退休後去讀神學，想做牧師。但我的父母，我的宗教老師，從沒要我成為信徒，他們讓我選擇。父親晚年時，我問過他《創世紀》的問題，他說不知道。他也許不是好的牧師，但我覺得這是誠實的答案。我尊重信男信女，但也要求他們尊重我可以相信其他。

美國 911 事件後，布殊認為不發達國家和地區佔全球八成人口，這些人口是垃圾，他們建立了「流氓國家」，令世界動盪不安。流氓一旦擁有大殺傷武器，那二成的精英可就糟糕了。他稱伊朗、伊拉克和北韓為三大「邪惡軸心」。然後我在電視看到外國一位著名的傳教士鼓吹攻打這些「邪惡軸心」。他來過香港，我在政府大球場聽過他的講道。《創世紀》裏洪水、天火，把異教徒都殺了，就解決問題麼？和平、公正，宗教能為我們帶來嗎？我也只能說：不知道。

世界至今的問題，仍然是老問題，霸道、一言堂、非黑即白、排他。

問：《孔林裏的駐校青蛙》中，不少詩作均談到恐怖主義、911、反恐等議題，最有趣是〈濟慈〉，把大詩人與恐怖分子相連，為甚麼會有此聯想？

何：這是這個時代的問題，濟慈是切入點，古今是可以打通的。

猶太裔的阿多諾說過，經過納粹奧斯威辛集中營，詩人要是還能寫詩讚美這個世界，那是不誠實，是野蠻的，是漠視人類的苦難。

他認為通過教育，消解權威性人格，奧斯威辛就不會重演。

現在看，奧斯威辛其實是以不同的形式重演，受害者可以反過來成為迫害者。詩人可以怎麼辦呢？如果他有武器，始終是語言，也只有語言。有一種無力感？文學藝術就有這種雙重性格，既置身於社會的權力網絡，又要擺脫現實社會的糾纏。他要顛覆舊世界、舊秩序麼，他本身就成為刺客。

問：〈審判〉與〈蘇格拉底受審〉分別書寫西方史上兩宗著名

的審訊，前者是文學的，卡夫卡的，後者是哲學的，希臘的，您認為這兩宗審訊，如何影響人類文明的發展？

何：〈審判〉令人想起卡夫卡，世事往往很卡夫卡。我讀孔子，想到蘇格拉底，讀柏拉圖、色諾芬、喜劇裏的蘇格拉底，也想到一些社會現象。至於如何影響人類文明的發展，是太大的問題，不能大題小做，我也沒有這個認識。

問：〈暴風雨來時〉是一首長詩，「向琉善（Lucian）致敬」之作，這位希臘語的諷刺作家，讀者或較為陌生，可否分享閱讀琉善的心得？

何：詩略長罷了，算不得長詩。琉善，又名盧奇安，生活在二千多年前，可說是古希臘最奇趣，最精彩的作家。他的《真實的故事》，分兩卷，近乎中篇小說，自述講的是老老實實的假話。他坐船出發，要探查大洋的盡頭。途經一個島，長滿葡萄樹，河水都是酒，葡萄樹長出女人來，被她們吻一下，就醉倒了。忽然大風把船捲到天上，成為飛船，就在天上航行。下望，是一個個浮島。然後，參加太陽和月亮爭逐霸權的星球大戰，原來太陽和月亮也有人居住，參戰的還有許多奇奇怪怪的大鳥、蒜頭軍、跳蚤弓箭手……，真是文字的狂歡節。又有夢幻島、睡眠港、惡人國；人老了，也不死，只化作一道青煙，例子舉不勝舉，想像非常豐富，戲謔，而且睿智、詼諧。這是西方文學嬉笑怒罵的傳統，像他說宴會旁的兩個泉眼，一口「笑泉」，一口「樂泉」。但不要以為他只是笑樂。實情是哭不得，所以笑。他不知何謂現代，更無所謂後現代。但後現代種種技法，他早就表演過了。

171

昆德拉説西方文學傳統，有一條很重要的路線，即「戲謔小説」（novel-as-game），可一直受忽略，一如「輕」和「重」兩條路線的發展。兩者其實是辯證的，卡爾維諾、格拉斯、魯西迪，都是輕重逢源的表表者。但輕的源頭，不是拉伯雷，而應該是琉善，他影響《巨人傳》、《堂·吉訶德》、《項狄傳》、《格列佛遊記》等等。別以為作家一口哭泉、一口苦泉，才是對人類文化的貢獻。《真實的故事》第二卷收結説：「至於那另一大陸的情況如何，且聽下卷分解」，古代抄寫人注云：「這是最大的謊言。」因為根本沒有下卷，那另一大陸是指他的故鄉。

勒瑰恩的名作《黑暗的左手》，也可以看到琉善對科幻的影響。琉善寫月亮的居民，生孩子的不是女人，而是男人，她們娶男人做妻子。根本沒有女人這個名詞。對了，二千多年後才有女性主義指出，「女性」是男性強加的標籤。男人二十五歲前出嫁做妻子，這年齡之後則娶親做丈夫。嬰孩出生，是在腿肚上，足月後切出死嬰，在風口上一吹，活過來了。我和西西談西方科幻小説，曾做過介紹。

《真實的故事》寫航行時被一條巨鯨吞進肚裏，鯨腹就是一個大城市，他們在鯨肚裏生活了好一陣。〈暴風雨來時〉就是從此而來。詩很普通，如果讓人多識人，多知書，哈哈，也不算白寫。

琉善，周作人譯過《盧奇安對話集》，是全譯了，他寫的對話，同樣有趣，在古希臘眾多的對話裏，也別開生面。羅念生等人譯出《琉善哲學文選》，另外水建馥曾譯出《真實的故事》，同樣譯自古希臘文，我最喜歡這個版本。

責任編輯：羅國洪
封面設計：余穎欣
內文插圖：余穎欣

愛在瘟疫時
Love in the Time of Coronavirus

作　　者：何福仁

譯　　者：Teresa Shen（沈鄧可婷）

出　　版：匯智出版有限公司
　　　　　香港九龍尖沙咀赫德道2A首邦行8樓803室
　　　　　電話：2390 0605　　傳真：2142 3161
　　　　　網址：http://www.ip.com.hk

發　　行：香港聯合書刊物流有限公司
　　　　　香港新界荃灣德士古道 220-248 號荃灣工業中心 16 樓
　　　　　電話：2150 2100　　傳真：2407 3062

印　　刷：陽光 (彩美) 印刷有限公司

版　　次：2021 年 4 月初版

國際書號：978-988-75441-3-5

香港藝術發展局全力支持藝術表達自由，本計劃
內容並不反映本局意見。